POISONOUS DEATH

JILL QUINT, MD FORENSIC PATHOLOGIST

ALEC PECHE

DEDICATION

This has been my get back in the writing saddle book. After a year of many life changes, I lacked the discipline and creativity to write. Two writing sprint groups helped me find my way back. Thank you Terry, Rachel, Peg, Dorajane, and Karen. Also thank you to Sisters in Crime for your timely writer sprints.

Once the story was complete, many thanks to first reader, GM Meyer, and editor Ellen Falk for fixing my sentence mistakes and timeline issues.

COPYRIGHT

Poisonous Death

CHAPTER 1

*J*ill Quint had just finished examining a row of dormant grapevines for signs of pests when her cell phone rang. She didn't recognize the number, so she figured it might be a spam call, but she never knew for sure as it was her personal number as well as the number for Dr. Jill Quint, Forensic Pathologist and Private Investigator.

"Hello, this is Jill."

"Hello, is this Dr. Quint?" came a reedy voice. Jill put the caller at an age of 80s or 90s.

"Yes, how may I help you?"

"I'm not sure that you can. My name is Catherine Dobson. My neighbor, Mary Niles, was found dead this morning. I think she was murdered. Can you help?"

Jill was missing a lot of basic information. How old was Mary? What did the local authorities think? Maybe they already knew they had a suspicious death. Why was a neighbor calling instead of a family member? Where to start with asking questions?

"Ms. Dobson, I have many questions for you before I can answer whether I can help. Does Mary have a family?"

"No. She never married, and her sister and niece predeceased her. She wrote a letter naming me as her spokesperson and executor and I did likewise, as I'm a widow."

Jill put her hand to her head thinking about what a huge headache this case might be. As a forensic pathologist, she had limited time that she could examine remains. She couldn't afford to wait a month or even a week if she was doing a forensic exam to look for poison.

"Why do you think your neighbor was murdered?"

"About a month ago, she started feeling unwell. She went to the doctor, but they couldn't find anything wrong with her."

"How were you notified that she passed?"

"We have tea together every morning. When I knocked on her door, there was no answer, and the door was locked, suggesting that she had not awoken yet. We both have emergency keys for each other's homes, so I got my key and went inside calling her name. I found her on the floor of her bedroom. She was cold to the touch and looked dead, but I called 9-1-1 anyway. They came and confirmed she was deceased and took her to our local mortuary as we had both made final arrangements with that company."

When she paused, Jill took a moment to ask her own questions. "I'm sorry for your loss. It sounds like you were close friends. How old was Mary?"

"She was eighty-five years young. She swam laps in the pool six days a week. She had no health issues other than a little arthritis in her hands. She was planning on another two decades."

"Where are you located?"

"We live in a city called Alviso, just north of San Jose."

"Did the police come?"

"Yes. They looked around and said, "It must be her time." They didn't find her death suspicious at all. They tried to console me instead of doing a little investigation. So I returned to my house and used my computer to figure out what to do next. I found your name and I called you."

Jill was so tempted to do what the police had done and call the situation a natural death, but one of the first cases she had ever handled as a private forensic pathologist had been an older client whose death was written off simply because of age.

Jill wondered if the woman could afford her fees. The San Francisco Bay Area was an expensive place to live, but that didn't mean that everyone was wealthy. She asked for the address and did a quick look-up and had her answer. Catherine would likely not be able to afford her services. The address was located inside a mobile home park, which was the only low-income housing source left in California. She quickly decided she would take the case on a pro-bono basis.

"Mrs. Dobson, can you send me the paperwork that says you are Ms. Niles' executor? I'm going to need it to get any answers from the authorities."

"Oh good. I'm so happy you'll help me find the answers. Mary shouldn't have died. I can take a picture of the paperwork and email it to you."

Jill provided her email address and made arrangements to visit Catherine in a few hours. She hoped the paperwork her client provided would be enough. Otherwise, she was going to face roadblocks to even talk to law enforcement, let alone perform an autopsy. Fortunately, in minimal traffic in the middle of the day, she would be there by one.

She called Nathan, her husband, to let him know of her new case. Her dog, Trixie, would be fine providing guard duty to her winery while she was away as she had a dog door and she could choose to stay in the house or chase squirrels outside. She loaded her car with her autopsy kit, grabbed an early lunch, and made the drive from California's central valley to the Bay Area. It was a beautiful drive through the Diablo Mountain range and past a windmill farm she could see from the highway. It was late November, so the hills were green with the recent rain.

She arrived in the city of Alviso by the appointed time. The city is at the base of the bay and often had an acrid stench of an unknown source. Residents theorized the smell originated in a local landfill or a water treatment plant, or from the fact that the water didn't turn over much and was prone to a wetland smell. Jill was lucky on this visit as the wind seemed to be blowing the other way. She entered a well-manicured mobile home park and found Catherine's home. Before knocking on the door, she turned and looked at the homes on either side speculating on which was Mary's home. She turned around and knocked.

The door was opened by a woman who was taller than Jill and likely an octogenarian. Jill held out her hand and said, "Ms. Dobson, I'm Dr. Jill Quint."

"Thank you for taking my call and responding so quickly. I hope you can find justice for Mary."

Jill was shown to a sofa in a comfortable living room. Catherine had a laptop sitting open on a coffee table and papers resting nearby.

"I'd like to see the paperwork that says you're to have control over Mary's estate upon her passing," Jill said. Catherine had emailed her the letter, but she wanted to see the original. Jill wasn't an attorney, but in this narrow area of the law, she was pretty sure she understood the requirements.

Catherine handed her the letter. Jill studied it, and though it was handwritten it was legible and notarized and contained the language that should help them in this case. She'd briefly glanced at the emailed document before she left, but it was good to confirm that it should work for this investigation. She nodded and then pulled out a contract for Catherine to sign. She was pleased to see her read the document and then sign it.

Once she finished, she looked over at Jill and said, "It

mentions compensation here. I can give you the proceeds from selling Mary's home, but not much else at this time. I'm an old legal secretary, so I've picked up a few things over the years."

"That's okay, Ms. Dobson. I decided to take on your case pro-bono when you first called. You're near my home, so I won't have travel expenses. Like you, I want justice for your friend. Early in my career as a private forensic consultant, I reviewed the case of another senior citizen that was thought to be a natural death. It was not, and someone is sitting in jail now for their crime. I think that is good news. We'll take a look at Mary and understand what caused her death and go from there. I assume that she is at the mortuary rather than the medical examiner's office because she was under the care of a doctor when she died. On my way here, I called the mortuary to stop them from doing anything with Mary, and I'll be examining her remains shortly. Tell me more about her feeling poorly in the past month. What were her symptoms?"

"She started feeling tired and for the first time in her life, her blood pressure was concerning. This puzzled her doctor as she said it was unusual to have high blood pressure for the first time in your 80s. Her doctor said most patients are diagnosed between 55 and 65 years of age."

"That's generally true, but there are reasons for blood pressure to rise, like kidney disease. Did she ever mention that?"

"No, she only had one doctor's visit since she began feeling poorly. That was when the high blood pressure was discovered. She was scheduled for a visit later this week."

"I need to leave to visit the mortuary. I'd like you to come with me as the request to involve me is unusual and I'll save time if you're there. I'll call a ride share service to take you home. After I examine your friend, I'd like to view her home, so I'll come back here."

"I need to meet with the mortuary folks and discuss the arrangements for the service. Although we already paid our fees and discussed our services with this mortuary, I'd like to arrange a celebration of life for our small community. We'll be moving in the next few months, so this will be one of the few final gatherings."

The way Mary made that statement, it sounded like all the residents were moving soon, which would be weird.

"Why are you moving?"

"Despite years of arguing in court, the mobile home park is being sold to a developer. The company plans to build condos overlooking the bay. So we all have to find a new place to live by the end of the year. Mary and I were actually going to leave the area as nothing is holding us in this town. We found a couple of options that we were going to make a decision about once Mary felt better."

Jill leaned over to give Catherine a hug. "You seem like you need a hug. Once we move beyond this case, I can help you find or make a decision on your next place to live."

Jill's offer made the older woman's eyes water. She said, "You're kind beyond what you need to be. Thank you."

"My mother lives in a senior community in Arizona. She's very happy and safe there. She's made new friends, which isn't easy considering she knew no one when she moved in and she's an introvert. I can set you up on a call if you want to hear from her the pros and cons of where she lives. I'm not saying you should move to Arizona, just that all senior communities likely have something in common."

"Actually, I'd appreciate hearing her thoughts as they may help me focus my search. Mary and I were down to three locations, but perhaps your mother could help me narrow it to one."

Jill nodded and waited for Catherine to gather a sweater and her purse before they left to walk toward her car. Jill followed Catherine's directions to the funeral home, and they entered. It took a good thirty minutes to establish Catherine's right to make decisions for Mary and then for Jill's credentials as a forensic pathologist to be accepted. The funeral home had never had a request for an autopsy to take place in their embalming area and discussed the issue with the medical examiner's office. In the end it was all cleared up. Jill was allowed to proceed with the autopsy and Catherine finished making her arrangements and returned home.

CHAPTER 2

*J*ill was searching her memory for the oldest person she'd been called to consult on in her history of giving second opinions on the cause of death. Mary Niles might be the oldest person; then she remembered the bus crash that she assisted the Sacramento medical examiner's office with and one of those victims might have been older. She decided that case didn't count, as there was no mystery as to why people died during the bus accident—it was blunt force trauma. Human bodies didn't like being flung about inside a bus.

She thought back to her days working for her local medical examiner and what she saw when she examined older remains. When a pathologist reviewed the remains of a twenty-something versus a seventy-something, things were different on the inside. The wear and tear of life was evident. If the person was a smoker or a heavy drinker, that was evident. Still, she would be able to tell if Mary's heart stopped beating as a result of a heart attack or an irregular beat. Despite news agencies reporting that a famous celebrity died from *natural causes*, there was actually no such thing. Over 60 percent of the people Mary's age died from organ failure—most often the heart. The heart just failed to keep beating. Over her lifetime, Mary's heart would have beat at least 3.6 billion times. It was bound to stop at some point. The second most likely organ to fail was probably the kidneys. Mary's symptoms showing up a month before she passed were indicative of one of these two organs failing.

Jill did her usual autopsy of examining and weighing the organs. She had no x-rays as Mary's remains didn't travel through a medical examiner's office. A funeral home would have no reason to have an x-ray machine in their possession. An x-ray would have allowed her to see broken bones, but it was extremely rare for a broken bone to cause death; instead, it was the infection in the bone or a blood clot caused by the break that caused death. Some tumors could be spotted on an x-ray, but if they were large enough to show on a regular x-ray and to cause a death, it was likely that Jill would spot them during her examination.

Two hours later she was sewing Mary's chest closed at the completion of her autopsy. Something was off and she hoped the chemical analysis that she planned to do once she reached her home would reveal something. If Mary's death was intentional, it wasn't obvious like a gunshot wound, a knife injury, or being hit on the head. She had a hard time determining the difference between wear and tear on organs versus poisoning of some kind. She returned Mary's remains to the care of the funeral home and was soon driving back to Catherine so she could have a tour of Mary's home. She had had Catherine put a hold on cremation just in case something came out of the autopsy and subsequent chemical analysis. The funeral home had storage space and Mary was in the cooler in case the medical examiner needed to get involved. She was reviewing the autopsy results from her memory during her drive back to the mobile home park. She would have a lot to examine once she arrived at her home lab in the Palisades Valley. In the interim, her specimen collections were on dry ice to preserve them until she could start processing them.

Jill pulled into Catherine's carport and got out of her car. Catherine must have heard her as she exited her front door carrying a key chain. Jill took a moment to look around at this housing community. She guessed that perhaps half of the homes were empty. She made a note to herself to ask more questions about that after she went through Mary's house.

"Did you find anything, Dr. Quint?" Catherine asked, once she walked over to Jill.

"Mary didn't die as a result of violence, or a stroke. I have a bunch of specimens to run when I return to my lab at home. I'm not ready to say Mary died of old age, but I can't be more definitive than that."

"Did everything look okay to you? Granted, I'm the same age as Mary and I imagine I have wrinkles on the inside to match those on the outside."

Jill smiled at Catherine's description and said, "As we age, we tend to see wear and tear on the organs. So it's not so much wrinkles as scars and clogged plumbing."

"That's a good way of explaining things," Catherine said as she unlocked the door to Mary's home.

"Show me where you found Mary and in what position," Jill requested, looking closely at Catherine to make sure she wasn't upsetting her. They were, after all, talking about her best friend and likely companion for many years. Catherine seemed to be handling things well as her friend's death wasn't entirely unexpected. She had called Jill almost on a whim. Still, Jill admired the older woman for her relationship with her late friend and how they made plans together. She could see Jo, Marie, and Angela likewise taking care of each other as they got older. She had Nathan, but the odds were that she would outlive him; she just hoped they had a very long future in front of them. If that didn't happen, and she suddenly found herself alone, she would likely sell her vineyard and move to Wisconsin to be with her friends. Enough with the morbid thoughts, it was time to focus on the case in front of her.

Jill and Catherine entered Mary's living room. Catherine said, "The kitchen is over there and that's where I found Mary lying on the floor."

"Was she lying on her side or her back?"

"Here, for some reason, I took a picture of her as I was waiting for the police to arrive."

Catherine shuffled through her pictures and showed Jill the one that she took that morning.

She looked at the picture and found Mary turned toward the left side, but mostly lying on her back.

"Can you send me a copy of that picture?"

"What's your email address? I didn't keep it after I sent you the paperwork this morning."

"Actually, let me make that easy and I'll just take a picture of your picture," Jill said, pulling out her cell phone and snapping a picture. Mary's position made her think that the woman had gotten up and gone to her kitchen and then felt lightheaded and slowly descended to the floor. It didn't help that much in diagnosing her cause of death.

She continued touring Mary's small home and then asked, "Do you know where Mary kept any prescriptions or other medications that she took regularly?"

Catherine showed her a medicine cabinet in the bathroom which contained aspirin, Pepto-Bismol, and other over-the-counter medications. Then they walked into the kitchen and Catherine opened a drawer where Mary kept her prescription medications. Jill wrote down the names of the medications as some of them might impact the lab results she was going to run that evening.

At the end of the tour, Jill did a quick video survey of the interior of the home. She likewise did the same outside. After a bit more conversation with Catherine, she left to return to her home lab and think about the death of Mary Niles as she sat in traffic leaving Silicon Valley.

CHAPTER 3

Jill had kept Nathan aware of her latest case and her approximate time for returning home that evening. He loved to cook and she loved to eat. It was one of many pleasures of being married to Nathan. He needed about a half-hour more preparation for their supper and she likewise needed the time to unload her specimens into her lab for processing later. Even though the dry ice kept things cold, she preferred her scientific refrigerator which accurately maintained a temperature conducive to the storage of specimens.

She walked inside and gave him a kiss and they exchanged pleasantries about their day. He was designing new art for one of his favorite winery clients. They wanted their art to reflect a fantasy story featuring warriors and dragons and wine. It was a new direction for Nathan, but he liked it. While he'd never sketched dragons on a label before, every wine label was a fantasy of sorts. Like book covers catching the eye of a reader, wine labels caught the imagination of the wine drinker searching for a bottle that might match their mood. Wine connoisseurs likely sniffed at the idea of buying a bottle based on the label—it should be about the quality of wine therein.

Still, research showed that upwards of 85 percent of people had purchased a bottle of wine based on the label, so Nathan's job as a wine label artist was as important as the winemaker's skill at creating a vintage.

After a delightful meal, she relayed more details about her case and a description of the friendship between Mary and Catherine. "After this case is over, I'll set up a conversation between Catherine and my mom. She can give Catherine her opinion of the pluses and minuses of 55-plus communities."

"Your client is lucky that she caught you at the right time. You haven't had a case in a few weeks, and with the complete sell-out of your latest vintage, you can afford to do a case pro-bono for her. It also helps that she's only a two-hour drive away when traffic is good," Nathan said.

"She is also lucky that one of my early cases as a private forensic investigator was of an elderly person that everyone assumed was a natural death. I have a soft spot for the prevention of elderly abuse. This woman was living a great life at 85. What's more, she had an excellent relationship with Catherine. That's so important in your later years. I hope Catherine can find a new friend once she moves as that will keep her healthier in the future. So yeah, this case, despite being a freebie. checks a lot of boxes on my checklist of helping the world be a better place."

Nathan leaned in to kiss her, saying, "The world is lucky to have you and so am I. I don't have such a checklist, and my daily work doesn't make the world a better place."

"Don't underestimate yourself. Remember all of those shoppers buying wine based on the label? You're making them happy when they spot your label. Think about it; you're more important to the purchase than the winemaker. You're helping small wineries like mine reach more customers and you help us earn coins to keep making more wine," Jill said with a smile. Then she stood up and asked, "Would you mind walking Trixie? I'm anxious to start processing my specimens. Something was off in her autopsy, and I can't put my finger on it. Or maybe it's a bias on my part that I don't want this active older woman to have died before what her friend perceived as her time."

"No worries, you go immerse yourself in your lab. I'll clean up and Trixie and I will head out for a walk. Do you want another glass of wine to take with you?" Nathan asked, holding up the wine bottle that accompanied their meal.

"Sorry to leave you with the dishes. I'll clean up the rest of this week. And no to more wine. While it was delicious, I need a clear head in my lab."

Jill left her house to cross the yard to her barn which was more a professional laboratory than a place for farm equipment and animals. She pulled out her routine autopsy checklist and got to work looking at her samples. Some tissues she would look at under a microscope, while others were blood samples that she would run through her analyzers. A few hours later, she had suspicious results. Mary had an unusually high level of arsenic in her blood. Her kidney tissue showed damage that was also likely due to arsenic. The poison was a natural element found in air, water, dirt, and even food.

The water that fed Mary's house was from the city of San Jose, so it should be safe; otherwise, there would be many more cases. She would ask Catherine to have her blood tested. If she went over to Mary's house for coffee or tea, then she might have been exposed, too. If it was in the air or dirt, again Jill thought there would be more cases. There had been recent food recalls of apple juice, rice cereal, and other rice products. Could Mary have drunk the bad apple juice? The timing was right with her onset of symptoms.

Many water wells supplied water unacceptably high in arsenic. In Bangladesh over 100 million people have been poisoned by arsenic-contaminated water. She looked at the time and decided it was too late to call Catherine. She had mentioned that the friends were early risers, so she was likely asleep. She looked at her pictures to see if there was any evidence of a water well, but she didn't see anything, but it could have been elsewhere in the community. Still, she was sure that the community didn't use a well for water. She went back to the house to see how Nathan was doing while mentally composing an email to her friends and teammates—Jo, Marie, and Angela. They enjoyed growing their vacation accounts with the fees they earned working on Jill's case, but given the story of Mary Niles, she was sure they would join this case. Helping Jill solve these cases also satisfied their own personal codes of justice.

When Jill re-entered the house, Nathan was working on his laptop with Trixie asleep at his feet, and Arthur curled up on the back of the sofa. Since they married and moved in together, the two enemies had somehow found peace between them. Mostly, it was detente with each animal, ignoring the existence of the other.

Nathan looked up from the screen and asked, "Did you find anything? You said there was something weird about Mary's remains, though you couldn't put your finger on it. And in your case, I guess that means literally."

"That was a good quip, Nathan. I did find something suspicious. Mary has toxic levels of arsenic in her blood. Arsenic can come from many sources, including food, air, soil, or water. I don't know if she accidentally came into contact with it or if someone poisoned her. I need to have another conversation with Catherine and advise that she get her blood tested for arsenic since the two women were so close and ate similar food, breathed similar air, and drank water from the same source. However, Catherine mentioned that she was a morning person, so I think it's too late at this point to call her."

"Are you going to call the police?"

"No, not yet. I need to know more about the source of the arsenic. Mary's remains are safe in the funeral home as Catherine, who has her power of attorney at the moment, asked that they not do anything other than preserve her remains at this point."

"Yikes. I didn't even think about what embalming fluid or a crematory furnace might do to one of your cases. It's a good thing your client called you as early as she did and that you were available to investigate."

"I think the world overall does a disservice to its seniors by not doing more autopsies to determine the cause of death. We would understand aging better, and we would probably get away from generic terms, like 'died of natural causes or died in their sleep,' which lack scientific rigor."

"At that interesting factoid, I'll leave you to head to bed while I do more design work here. My ideas are flowing, and I don't want to stop just now."

"I'm just going to compose an email to Jo, Marie, and Angela. I may need their help tomorrow, and even though this isn't a paid gig, I think they'll want to join the case."

"Yes, I think they will," Nathan said distractedly. Jill smiled as she could tell this was one of those moments where most of his brain was focused on a design, and he could barely hold a conversation with her. It was one of the things she loved about him—he could get so deeply immersed in his work.

She grabbed her tablet and went upstairs to their bedroom. Minutes later she was propped up on pillows composing her email to her friends. The case wasn't a confirmed homicide yet, so the email was just a heads-up that she might need them to help in the next day or so. She described the case and added in the friendship between the two women, its pro-bono status, and what she found so far. With the time difference between California and Wisconsin where her three friends lived, she had no expectation that anyone was awake in that state to read her email. Still, she liked to summarize a case while her thoughts were fresh.

She gave details about the mobile home park and its future scheduled demolition. She also summarized the region and value of the land in that location. Finally, when she ran out of details to describe the case, she moved on to some notes that she wanted to make sure she covered with Catherine when she spoke with her in the morning. With everything wrapped up, she fell asleep after setting aside her laptop.

CHAPTER 4

$\mathcal{A}$s always Jill awoke before Nathan. Today they wouldn't see much of each other. He was heading to the university, where he taught a class in wine branding. He would stay overnight there and teach another class the next day and then return home. Jill looked at the time and decided she could call Catherine as it was now after seven in the morning.

"Hello?"

"Hi, Catherine. This is Jill Quint. From what you said yesterday, you're a morning person, so I hope it's not too early to call you."

"Good heavens, yes. I've had my breakfast and am nearly finished with my second cup of tea. Did you find anything with your analyzers last night?"

"As a matter of fact, I did. However, what I found is not yet proof that your friend was murdered. I'll need to look at a few more things. Where does the water in your house come from? Do you pay the city for your water?"

"That's a strange question. Yes, I get a monthly water bill from the city. What's this got to do with Mary?"

"I found a dangerous level of arsenic in Mary's blood. . . ."

Jill was cut off from her explanation by Catherine's "Oh my! She was poisoned! Who would do that?"

"Catherine, let me explain. Arsenic is a naturally occurring element in the air, water, soil, and food we eat. Thus my first question about your water source. Water wells are notorious for having high levels of arsenic. I think you should have your blood tested for the element. If you and Mary spent a lot of time together, you may have been exposed to it as well. There was a recall on apple juice a few weeks ago as it was contaminated with arsenic. So just finding an abnormal level of arsenic in her blood is more about what killed her than a statement that it was murder. Do you understand?"

"Yes. I haven't had any of the symptoms that Mary had for the past month, so I doubt I was exposed. Why didn't Mary's doctor find the arsenic in her blood?"

"That's a good question, but my guess is because when you look at a collection of symptoms in someone Mary's age, and wonder about their cause, arsenic poisoning doesn't rate in the top ten potential diagnoses. I would likely think of heart or kidney problems or perhaps an infection. Does my explanation make sense? Look, I need to come to your park and test the water in Mary's trailer. Why don't we chat face to face in a little more than two hours?"

"Thank you, Dr. Quint. I would appreciate that. As you can imagine, I'm dismayed with what you're telling me about Mary's death."

Jill gathered the supplies she would need to test Mary Niles' water and set forth to meet with Catherine.

She knocked on Catherine's door once she arrived in the mobile home park. When the door opened, she asked, "Catherine, how are you doing?"

Catherine looked sad and said, "I don't know whether to be mad or sad that I lost my best friend to arsenic."

"It's okay to be both. I'm more concerned about you at the

moment. I'm worried you may also have arsenic poisoning. I assume you spent considerable time near Mary and therefore you have likely been exposed to whatever the source of arsenic is. Does that make sense?"

"Yes, it makes sense. How do I get my blood tested? I'm afraid if I called my doctor and asked for an arsenic test, that she might prescribe some anti-anxiety medication or something."

Jill let out a small laugh at Catherine's comment. "I maintain my license as a physician in the state of California, so if you tell me which lab you normally use, I'll give them a call and place a physician's order for the blood test." She liked that Catherine was a fast thinker and she was impressed with her brain given the grief she must feel over the demise of her best friend.

Catherine found the phone number for her local lab and gave it to Jill. A few minutes later the arsenic test was authorized.

"Do you need Mary's key while I run to the lab?" Catherine asked.

"Yes. I plan to look around her home for the source of the arsenic. I have a kit with me that will allow me to test her home for the element."

Catherine nodded and went inside her kitchen for the key. Jill wondered briefly how Catherine got around. She didn't see a car near her home, and she knew that many people gave up driving at a certain age. As she was entering Mary's home, she saw a senior transportation service car pause outside her home. She felt relieved to see Catherine leave and get her blood tested. She went back to her search. She started with the kitchen faucet. She turned the water on and tested it. It came back positive for arsenic. She paused to look up the telephone number for the water company and dialed.

She got passed around and then ended up in a quality area. Once she had an analyst on the line, she explained the situation and, in particular, Mary's death from arsenic poisoning. They promised to send someone out immediately. Jill continued to test liquids in the house and refrigerator and cups in the dishwasher. She found evidence in the cups in the dishwasher which likely meant that Catherine was exposed as well. She'd wait for the lab test results and if it came back positive, she would call Catherine's physician to explain the situation.

With nothing more to do, she looked around the home. Mary had lots of yarn and crochet needles. She also had a thick file on the sale of their mobile home park. Jill looked at the dates on the paper in the file and found that Mary had been fighting against losing her home for four years. She must have loved living in this home.

Jill heard a sound outside and saw that it was Catherine getting out of the senior transportation service car. She went outside to invite her into Mary's home while she was waiting for the water company to arrive.

"The lab told me that my results would be available in four to six hours and that they would call you with the results. Did you find the source of the arsenic in Mary's house?"

"I did find the source. It's coming out of Mary's kitchen faucet. The water company is on their way here to investigate. You said you had tea each morning with Mary. Did you drink water from this house at any other time?" Jill said, then thought of something else. "Let's go over to your house and let me test the water there."

Catherine looked anxious at that thought, but nodded and led the way. They walked straight to her kitchen sink and Jill pulled out her test kit. She was relieved for Catherine to find no arsenic detected. However, the mystery of Mary's death deepened with Jill finding her next-door neighbor's water to be free of arsenic.

"This is strange. As far as I know this entire community gets its water from the same source. We could look at the pipes and

Mary's house, but arsenic is usually not found in water pipe metals. This will be a mystery for the water department to solve."

"So the drinking water in my house is safe? Typically, I only drank one cup of tea with Mary each morning. I know she had a water bottle that she filled from the faucet and of course she cooked with that water. Does boiling water get rid of arsenic?" Catherine asked.

"No. Boiling water gets rid of harmful bacteria, but you can't boil off an element like arsenic. So your tea would have contained arsenic."

Catherine looked worried and was glad that Jill had arranged the blood test for her. She wondered if she would start feeling ill like Mary had for the past month.

They heard a noise outside and noticed a truck with the insignia of the water company had arrived. Jill gathered up her test kit and went outside to chat with the two staff members.

"Hello, I'm Dr. Jill Quint and I called you to report the water in this home," she said, pointing to Mary's house. "I just tested the water in this house, and it came back clean for arsenic," she added, pointing to Catherine's house.

The two technicians introduced themselves and gathered up their own test kit to follow Jill and Catherine into Mary's house. There was silence in the kitchen as they watched the technicians test the water and the faucet. They were soon frowning over the results.

"This is dangerous. We need to shut the water off to this home. Did you say that the owner passed away yesterday?" the technician named Dave asked. "We need to confirm your test on the other house so we know how many homes here have unsafe water."

"As I mentioned on the phone, I'm a consulting forensic pathologist. I did an autopsy yesterday on the woman who lived here, and I ran chemistry tests on her blood last night in my home lab in Pleasant Valley. That blood came back for a high level of arsenic," Jill said as they walked over to Catherine's home. She observed the technicians coming back with the same data she had.

They returned outside of the two homes and one of the technicians grabbed a water meter valve key, which was a heavy pipe with a U at the end of it and looked around Mary's home for the meter. Then he frowned and asked his coworker, "What's this?"

Jill and Catherine followed Dave over to the water meter and looked at what his coworker was pointing to. There was a little pipe between the meter elbow and the house. The two water techs decided to remove the thing from the meter. Then Jill had a thought.

"Excuse me, would you allow me to call the police first? We may have a homicide on our hands and there could be fingerprints on that pipe thing."

The two workers flung their hands upward as though the pipe was hot. They stood up and backed away and then had a discussion. Dave said, "We'll wait here until the police arrive. We may have touched the pipe and I guess they'll want our fingerprints to eliminate those from anyone else's on the pipe. Meanwhile, we'll put a note on all the sinks, as well as the door so that no one drinks the water in this house."

Jill nodded and placed a call to the police. It took her a while to get connected to the detective division. She knew from her time working in the medical examiner's office that police got their fair share of crank calls. Usually once she explained her credentials and directed an officer or a detective to a news story on one of her cases, they paid attention to her story. They said they would respond and be on the scene within 20 minutes. She sat down on the steps of Mary's house and began composing an email to her friends. She also let Nathan know she might be detained. As this was his night to stay near the university, it wouldn't matter when she arrived home. This case had all the appearances of a homicide, but the police and the official medical examiner would have to make that declaration.

Catherine had returned inside her house due to the fall chill. The water department workers were sitting in their utility truck waiting for law enforcement to arrive. Jill bet that the two workers were having a fascinating conversation about potentially their strangest day ever at work. She looked up when she heard a noise and saw a car approaching. It was unmarked, but she thought it was probably her detective arriving on the scene. The car drove up to the house and parked next to Mary's carport. A woman exited the car carrying a notepad. Jill could see the badge pinned to her belt and stood up to greet her.

CHAPTER 5

"Hello, detective. I'm Dr. Jill Quint, a forensic pathologist who provides second opinions on the cause of death. I was called to examine the remains of the occupant of this home," Jill said, pointing to Mary's house. "Her friend, Catherine Dobson, had found her deceased yesterday morning. Given Mary's age of 85 and the fact that she was under the care of a doctor, she was thought to have died of natural causes. Catherine has power of attorney rights for Mary and called me for a second opinion. I performed an autopsy on Mary at the funeral home yesterday. I took a variety of speci mens and blood samples home to process in my home lab in the Central Valley. I discovered a heavy dose of arsenic in Mary's blood. As you may or may not remember from your training, arsenic is in the air, the water, the soil, and sometimes in the food we eat. This morning, I arrived at Mary's house to see if I could determine where the arsenic came from. Perhaps she had a bottle of apple juice that was recently recalled for arsenic contamination. However, I hit the jackpot first when I tested the water coming out of the faucet in her kitchen. I then went to Catherine's house and tested her faucet, and it was negative. As

Catherine routinely drank tea with Mary inside this house, I sent her out for a blood test for arsenic. Meanwhile I called the water department to report my findings. They arrived and performed the same test that I had and proceeded to go to the water meter and turn it off. Once there, they discovered a foreign object in the water supply. At that point I called you."

"I'm Detective Robin Greenwood. This might be the most unusual story I've heard in my career. I did a quick search of your illustrious career, Dr. Quint. As you can imagine, your call sort of sounded like a crank call. Now that I know the rough details of the case, I want to get the crime scene crew here and then interview the neighbor, yourself, and the water department employees."

The detective stepped away to make her phone call. Five minutes later she was back, with pen and paper ready to take more notes. She'd made a quick stop at the workers' truck asking them to stay on scene if possible. Then she approached Jill.

"Would you take me to the neighbor that found Mary Niles deceased?"

"Sure, follow me," Jill said, walking toward Catherine's home. She went up the two steps and knocked on the door. A short time later the door opened and they were escorted into the living room. Jill was somewhat surprised that the detective didn't excuse her from this interview, as Catherine was the witness who found Mary on the floor yesterday and could describe her life.

The detective asked questions about the condition and position that she found Mary in when she entered her home the previous day. They were all the same questions that Jill had already asked. Then she moved on to learn more about Mary Niles—family, activities, etc.

She then asked a question that Jill hadn't, "Did Mary have any enemies? Were you aware of anyone who disliked her?"

"Mary was angry that an investor was allowed to buy this mobile home park and force all of us residents to relocate. She and I had considered these homes our forever homes. She found a couple of free legal resources to fight the investor, and that battle has been going on for nearly five years. Sadly, the investor finally won, and we have to move by the end of the year. We never met this investor personally, but I think they would be angry over the delays that Mary caused them."

"How about the residents in this community? Were there any arguments between residents? Was someone making too much noise or parking the wrong way?" Detective Greenwood asked.

There was silence in the room while Catherine thought about the answer to the question. Then she shook her head and said, "No. Everyone who lived in this community had been here for at least a decade. If you didn't get along, you moved out of here."

"Do you remember if any of the residents who moved out disliked Mary or disagreed with her fighting the sale?"

"Residents would not get mad at other residents. The property manager here was a strict disciplinarian and any resident who left would have been far more likely to target the manager than Mary."

The detective collected Catherine's contact information and stood up to leave her home. Jill eyed Catherine, assessing how she was holding up. She would be an emotional wreck if she lost her closest friend, but perhaps beyond a certain age you lose many friends to death and disease and so handle it better.

They exited Catherine's home, and the detective was going to ask Jill additional questions, but a crime scene van rolled up. The detective asked Jill to take a seat while she discussed the case with her techs. As she was walking away, Jill called out to the detective, "Hey Detective, you may want to make a call to the funeral home to make sure they leave Mary's remains untouched. I requested that yesterday, but you have more pull than I do. I know you're not close to officially labeling the case as a homicide, but I wouldn't want the funeral home to accidentally tamper with the evidence."

She nodded and pulled out her phone to make a quick call to what Jill presumed was the funeral home. Jill sat down on a chair outside of Catherine's house. She did a search for the item that was sitting in line with the water pipe. They had no proof that it contained arsenic, but it was suspicious. She lost herself in the search and missed some of the activity taking place. She joined the crime scene folks, the detective, and the water department experts as they opened up the pipes. It was a good thing that no one was living there any more as the home would be out of water for the foreseeable future. Judging from the black dust on the pipe, it was already checked for fingerprints. The prints were a long shot as who knew how long the pipe had been there, and people potentially would have handled it at the store where it was purchased.

She watched as the water department technicians used pipe saws to cut away the section containing the unknown pipe. They handed it to the crime scene techs who were wearing gloves. The group walked over to a table and she watched them photograph the item and then begin reaching inside for something that was in the pipe. Using the largest set of needle-nose pliers that Jill had ever seen, the crime scene techs pulled out what looked like a filter of sorts. It was much bigger than the coffee filter in her k-cup machine. There was silence as the filter was tested for arsenic. It came back positive.

The detective asked of anyone who knew the answer, "Is this enough arsenic to kill a human being?"

"It depends on the length of time that your victim drank from it. From what I heard, the resident hadn't been feeling good for a month before she passed yesterday," Dave said.

"It certainly wouldn't kill anyone in a day or two. Arsenic is an element, and it can build up in your kidneys and cause damage there as well as to the heart. I wonder when the filter was placed in this pipe. Let me ask Catherine if she remembers anyone from the water department visiting this community recently." Jill held her fingers up in quotation marks when she said "water department" as that filter did not come from the real water department.

"The presence of this filter is causing me to label this case as suspected homicide. I'll have Mary's remains moved to the medical examiner's office for a report. Dr. Quint, I would appreciate it if you would send me copies of all the work you've done so far," the detective said.

With the police stepping into the case and it being a likely homicide, Jill's work was essentially done. She could stop her investigation now and Catherine would be comforted by the fact that the police were involved. Still, she was going to put some research into the case just to make sure the murderer was caught. He or she almost got away with it, and they would have if not for the call that Catherine made.

Jill walked over and knocked on Catherine's door. It was good news and bad news. The good news was that Mary's murderer wasn't going to get away with it; the bad news was that she was murdered at all. Catherine invited her in.

"How are you holding up? It's been an extremely stressful two days for you."

"I'm alternating between being mad and being sad. Mostly I'm mad that it's starting to look like Mary's death was not due to natural causes. Has that detective found anything new?"

"She has. She has declared Mary's death a potential homicide. There's something in the water pipe going into her home that was added by somebody. That piece of additional pipe contains a filter full of arsenic. That's pretty damning evidence of malicious intent."

Catherine's eyes watered at the confirmation that her best

friend's death wasn't a matter of just being her time to die. Someone had taken years away from Mary and from their friendship.

"The detective will be asking you this question, but I thought I would get you thinking about it—have you noticed any vehicles in the area with the insignia of a plumbing company or a water company, say, in the last month to six weeks?"

It seemed that by asking Catherine questions it helped dry up her tears and focused her on what she could do for Mary now that Mary was no longer around to help herself. She got that look in her eyes like she was searching for a memory but was blind to her living room. Jill waited patiently for her response.

"I do remember a plumbing truck perhaps two months ago. I remembered it because I hadn't seen a plumbing truck in this neighborhood for a couple of years. I wondered if one of the unoccupied homes had sprung a leak. However, that was just a quick thought that passed through my mind as I went about my day. I don't think I could give you a description of the vehicle or even if the driver was male or female. You might ask the manager about any repairs in the community. He tends to be on top of things."

"That's a good suggestion, Catherine. I wonder if his office has any video cameras monitoring the property. The manager would also know if there was a legitimate plumbing repair or if none of the homes here had sprung leaks recently."

Jill felt a vibration from her cell phone and glanced down at it. It was an email from the lab that she had sent Catherine to. She paused in her conversation to open and read the email.

"I just received your lab result for arsenic. You have an elevated level, but generally not one that is clinically significant. I'll forward the result to your physician. It should clear out of your system within the week and since we've discovered the source of the arsenic and removed it, you won't have any additional exposure."

Catherine nodded, seemingly relieved to know that she wouldn't be suffering from arsenic poisoning.

"The detective is moving Mary from the funeral home to the medical examiner's office. They've asked for copies of my work and likely will be repeating it themselves. The police have opened an investigation into Mary's death. I don't know that there's a lot more I can do for you or Mary now that the police are on the scene."

Catherine looked pained and asked, "Do you have to leave the case? If it wasn't for you, no one would ever know that Mary had been murdered."

"Catherine, that's actually a tribute to you. You were sure that Mary was a healthy 85-year-old and you went to the trouble of finding me on the Internet. If you hadn't done that, no one would ever have noticed the extra pipe in the water line outside of Mary's house. Instead, it would have been covered up when this community is demolished for new construction. I also like that you called me right away. If the funeral home had prepared Mary's body for burial or for cremation, that would have interfered with the tests. You need to take credit for seeing that your best friend shouldn't have died when she did, and then you did something about it. Mary was lucky to have you as a friend."

"Your mother raised an amazing daughter. For someone who's spent a lot of time around dead bodies, you have quite the touch with us living people. Thank you for the kind words. You never asked for payment and even if you had, I wouldn't have been able to come up with much to pay you. Still, if you have time and don't mind doing some more free work, I'd love for you to stay on the case and find Mary's killer. I have faith in the police, but you've been so much faster. I'm worried that it's going to take them a long time to process fingerprints and other things that they collected here. They talk about the backlogs in big-city mortuaries, so I'm not even sure when they'll get around to autopsying Mary."

Jill thought about Catherine's request. She had admitted to herself that this was a very curious case. If not for the close friendship between these two women, a homicide would have gone unrecognized. It bothered Jill that society was so quick to decide that seniors were dying of natural causes. She sometimes wondered what the actual death rate was in Mary's age group. She made up her mind to do her share.

"I'll continue looking into this case. I already shared with my teammates the broad strokes of the case. Like me, they'll likely want to continue to find Mary the justice she deserves. We don't think the police are incompetent, but the four of us can focus on Mary's case alone—we don't have multiple murder cases that we're trying to research. Also, my friends are experts in following the money or following what people have said on social media. Sometimes that's a resource the police don't have on a particular case. I'll keep you posted with what we find. On another note, I spoke with my mother regarding your situation, and she'd love to help you with her thoughts on the pluses and minuses of senior communities. She asked that I give you her phone number so you can set up a time to chat. Will that work for you?"

Catherine smiled and said, "Yes, I would appreciate speaking with her. I'll call her and set up a time to talk. Thank you, Dr. Quint, and keep me informed. I have a feeling that the detective is not going to do a good job keeping me informed since I'm a friend, and not family."

"Don't hesitate to show her your power of attorney document to remind her that you are Mary's family," Jill said, before leaving Catherine's house.

She walked over to the detective and said, "I'm going to head home now. I'll send you all the data I have in an email once I get there. Just a reminder that Catherine Dobson is Mary's legal next of kin and she deserves to be updated on your investigation. She was the person who got the ball rolling to prove her friend hadn't died of natural causes. Is there anything else I can do for this investigation?"

Detective Greenwood thought about saying something and then decided to let it go, Jill thought watching the detective's face. She might have been annoyed with Jill over her mention of her duty to Catherine, but Jill didn't care—Catherine needed friends to look out for her. Instead, the detective nodded, and Jill turned away to walk to her car for the drive home.

CHAPTER 6

*J*ill arrived home mid-afternoon to an empty house. Nathan was teaching today and tomorrow at the university. She liked to give Arthur, Nathan's cat, a little extra attention when he was gone. Trixie, her Dalmatian, gave her a look of sorrow whenever Arthur claimed her attention. Arthur did his best to constantly barrage the dog with looks of superiority.

She fixed herself a late lunch and took it with her out to the lab to prepare to send an information packet to the detective. That task completed, she turned her attention to her email and smiled. All of her friends indicated a willingness to work for free to find a senior woman's killer. She loved that they had each taken a different angle on the case. Jo was looking into the finances of the mobile home community and the investor, whose name was HBZ Builders, headquartered in Southern California. Marie was examining the social media posts of Mary, Catherine, and their community and the history of the sale of their mobile home park. Angela did her best work in person, but was on standby to contribute to the case if needed.

Jill gave her friends an update on the case, including the

involvement of the police. She also mentioned Catherine asking them to stay on the case and her agreement to do so. She wrote in her email that she was going to do research to see if there were other deaths in other mobile home parks that appeared to be of natural causes. That accomplished, she did a walk around her vineyard as it was a never-ending source of work, and it allowed Trixie to stretch her legs. She then returned to the house and began her research into elderly deaths. She barely touched the data on the subject after many hours of research. It was time to let it go for the day and get back to her other business—making wine.

After a murder investigation that had taken her to Sicily, Italy, Jill came home with the plan to plant the Nero d'Avola red grape plant to begin making a second varietal after her success with Moscato. She harvested her first crop of the new grape last year, and it had been fermenting. With Moscato, she didn't need to age the wine in oak barrels before it was to be bottled for sale. However, the Nero d'Avola grape required one to two years of aging. This was her third monthly tasting of the aging wine barrel, and she was excited to taste it. When she was in Sicily for the case, she and her friends tasted roughly thirty different vintages. They generally agreed with her on the best bottle and so she thought she was on to something. She went outside to one of her barns where she stored the wine.

When she planted the new grape, she remodeled one of her barns to account for the barrels. She created a subterranean room, which was cooled with a geothermal HVAC system. The wine barrels needed to be kept at 45-55 degrees Fahrenheit, and Pleasant Valley was hot. The Muscat grape which created Moscato wine liked a hot and dry climate like that in California's Central Valley. The Nero d'Avola grape likewise liked the heat to grow in, but it needed cooler conditions to age in. The wine barrel room was a pleasure to walk into on a hot summer day. Year round, she loved the smell of wine that permeated the room.

Walking into the cool room brought back memories of her first teenage job—she worked for a fast-food burger joint and had to cut onions for burgers. Her eyes would water as long as she was slicing, and she would go into the walk-in refrigerator to cool down her eyeballs from the onions. She supposed that nowadays they had a machine that sliced and diced the onions, so some poor food service worker was no longer crying through their shift.

She walked over to the testing barrel and undid the cap. She stuck her wine thief inside to withdraw a sample. The wine thief was a glass pipette that sucked up wine. She dropped the liquid into a wine glass and swirled it around the glass and sniffed the bouquet. She was satisfied with the bouquet and could remember how it had smelled at her previous tasting. She thought this was an improvement. She then swallowed her first mouthful, savoring the flavors in the wine. Her question of the moment was, is this the best this wine can be? Or should it age more before bottling?

After a second pipette's worth of the wine, she decided her wine was perfect. She would open the remainder of the barrels and confirm they were ready. If they were ready, she would reserve a mobile wine-bottling trailer. At the longest, she wanted no more than two weeks to pass before the wine was bottled. It was beyond the height of the harvest season, so she didn't anticipate problems with getting the bottler to her vineyard on time. Nathan had already created a label for her, so she was all set to go. She liked the boring work of filling and labeling bottles. It was the final step in bringing her grapes to someone's palate. Her local wine store, which routinely sold out of her Moscato vintage, was on standby to sell this new wine. She had a miniature wine bottle that she would fill using her wine thief. Then she would take it to the owner and get his opinion. Sometimes that was the most nerve-racking moment in her production.

Wine was such a personal preference. She'd had expensive, well-rated wine that she didn't want to waste the calories drinking as it didn't appeal to her palate. She'd also had a few bottles of two-buck Chuck, the nickname given to wine sold by Trader Joe's for $1.99, and the vintner was Charles Shaw. The question was whether she was creating a tasty vintage that the majority of people would like enough to buy a second bottle. She took her sample and headed into town to the wine merchant. After pouring them each a glass, she turned away to watch the customers in the store, barely breathing as she awaited his verdict.

"Jill, I should be able to sell this. It's one of the best Nero d'Avolas that I have ever tasted. It's not a varietal that many people ask for, but they do ask for Italian wines and many red drinkers are looking for something new."

Jill relaxed and smiled, relief coursing through her at his pronouncement. "I should have about 1,500 bottles within two weeks. How many bottles or cases would you like?"

"I'll start with nine cases. I'd also like to refer you to a wine merchant in the city who loved your Moscato vintage and wanted to try anything else you created."

"Wow, that's excellent news! Give me his contact information and I'll make an appointment." Jill soon left the store with the contact information in hand.

She made an appointment with the wine merchant in San Francisco for the next day. The mobile bottling truck would be onsite the following Tuesday to process her wine barrels. Since she was by herself for dinner, she pulled out some frozen leftovers from Nathan's cooking. She would have an excellent meal, and she wouldn't be eating junk food. She sat down to eat and started going through her emails.

Of course, her friends were all in on researching the case as they wanted to find justice for Mary Niles. She opened Jo's email first. Jo was just scratching the surface. She said there was a lot of concerning information about the building company HBZ builders. They were a large company with projects in California and the Southwest. Jo understood that trailer parks were one of the last low-income forms of housing left in California. She said she was getting heartburn reading about the number of trailer parks that were converted into luxury condos. She wanted Jill to know she was fascinated by the research required for this case.

Well, if her team lacked the money motivation of this case, at least the research made it interesting. She hoped that Marie and Angela would come to the same conclusion.

She moved on to Marie's email. Mary Niles was quite the rabble rouser. She'd managed to link up with a few groups to fight against the sale of their park. One group was a tenants' rights group, while another dealt with elder abuse, and the final group tried to prove that the trailer park owner didn't have the right to sell the land under each of their trailers. Mary had kept the park from being sold for over five years. However, she realized about ten months ago that she and all the other residents were going to lose. The court case was finally settled mid-year, and the park would be demolished by the New Year. The one thing Mary's lawsuit did do for the residents was increase the payment they received for their homes.

Mobile homes could be bought and sold and were the only housing type left in Silicon Valley under half a million dollars. The owners of the home paid monthly rent for the land the home sat on. Those rents averaged $700-$1700 a month depending on a number of factors. Mary's fight netted the remaining residents of the park half a million for the loss of their property and land as part of the settlement with the builder-investor. While the amount sounded generous, the average home in that area was over one million dollars. All of the mobile park residents that sold their homes in the past two years left Silicon Valley as they didn't have enough money to afford a new house in the area. It was very disruptive for many seniors who lived in the park—it wasn't easy moving your primary residence in your 70s and 80s. A few community members were mad at Mary, blaming her for a variety of issues. They thought her actions would reduce the price they got for the sale of their trailer from the investor. Other community members were afraid the investor was negotiating with Mary on their behalf. It was all nonsense, but not unexpected during the stressful time of having to move.

So all of Jill's friends were mad at the circumstances that a lot of these trailer park residents found themselves in, and that was good. That meant that they would be staying on the case with her. It was also concerning that Mary Niles' situation was increasingly becoming familiar to trailer park residents. It seemed like there should be a law that after you spend several hundred thousand dollars on a trailer, the land can't be sold underneath it for some time like thirty or fifty years. Oh well, that problem was for legislators, not for her to solve.

Jill got an email from her mother regarding the lovely conversation she had had with Catherine Dobson. Her mother thought she had assisted Catherine mostly by confirming that the choice she was making was indeed the right choice. Jill's mom said they were planning to stay in touch and that she was proud of Jill for solving the murder of Catherine's friend. She didn't always understand the technical medical jargon that was Jill's second language, but she understood that Jill had uncovered the death of someone who shouldn't have died. Jill wrote back to say that all she'd done was determine that Catherine's best friend was murdered; she hadn't solved who did it.

It had been an eventful day. Jill was always satisfied when her work laid the evidence for the police to get involved in a case. She was confident that even without the help of law enforcement, she could solve the case. While she might be able to determine who the murderer was, she lacked the power to arrest and charge someone. And frankly, she didn't want that responsibility.

She decided it was time to hit the sack and after a phone conversation with Nathan, she settled into a blissful sleep.

CHAPTER 7

Jill had a mid-morning appointment with the wine merchant in San Francisco. She collected a new sample of her Nero d'Avelo wine to take to the merchant. She also had a meeting with Detective Greenwood as she had something she wanted to discuss. Jill packed her findings about Mary Niles' autopsy just in case the detective had any questions about her findings. She took Trixie for a run and gave Arthur a good ear rub. Both pets settled in for a nap as she left the house.

As with the day before, Jill held her breath while she awaited the verdict from the wine seller. She left twenty minutes later with an order for another ten cases. She thought about her delivery process as she ventured outside of her home city to sell her wine. She could acquire a small delivery vehicle outfitted with a refrigeration unit so that her wine didn't spoil in the heat of a summer delivery. Of course it was fall now, heading into winter, so she didn't have to worry about the temperatures for now. Delivery would be something to solve for her winery later. Her mind moved on from wine to murder as she set her car's navigation for the SJPD.

Forty minutes later she was in the lobby waiting for Detective Greenwood to escort her to her division. The building on the outside was a boring concrete, blah-looking building. The inside was crowded with people there for various inquiries. Jill decided to lean against the wall and watch people, trying to figure out why they were there. She had never been inside a police department for personal reasons; it was always due to a case. The detective exited a door in the waiting room and invited Jill inside.

"Is your waiting room always that busy? I don't think I have seen that inside other police stations that I've been in."

"Yes, it's often that busy. Despite the fact that you can file a report online, many citizens want to do it in person. I don't know if they think we'll pay more attention to an in-person filing, but we don't. It's a manpower issue, and there are some small crimes that we won't ever get to investigating."

The detective directed her into a conference room that had two other people. Detective Greenwood performed introductions.

"This is my partner, Detective Susie Crawford, and Supervising Criminalist Jordan Currey. This is Dr. Jill Quint, Forensic Pathologist, and Private Investigator."

Jill looked at the detective, she hadn't mentioned to her that she had her P.I. license as her role in this case was due to her forensic pathology skills. The detective must have done a search on her. Oh well. Hopefully that meant that she knew how helpful Jill and her team could be. Jill shook hands with Crawford and Currey and took a seat.

"Our medical examiner confirmed your test results of an arsenic level likely the result of the inline water filter at her home. We don't have all the other tests available and won't for a few weeks, but Mary Niles' death is officially a homicide."

Jill nodded, having no expectation of anything else given the early evidence in the case. "Have you informed Catherine Dobson? She's Mary's power of attorney."

"No. I'll take care of that after this meeting. I want to interview her some more."

"Yes. She said Mary hadn't been feeling well for the past month and had visited her physician, but no diagnosis was made. Did you get any fingerprints off the arsenic filter?"

"Just the water company guys."

"It was never going to be that easy. How about cameras in the area? Was anyone caught on camera?"

"Management did away with the monthly cost of security cameras knowing that the community would be vacated in another sixty days or so. So again, nothing so easy," said the detective.

"How about the arsenic filter? Were you able to track that down?"

"No. It was rather ingenious. The murderer took a standard water filter, removed the charcoal out of the filter, and put arsenic powder inside. According to our crime lab, it was the perfect level of coarseness—it didn't dissolve in water immediately, rather, a toxic amount was used each time water was pulled from the pipe. We also found the soil outside where Mary watered her plants to be rich in arsenic."

"So she would have swallowed arsenic in her tea and in whatever she cooked as boiling water concentrates arsenic. If she washed fruits or vegetables, they would be contaminated with the element."

Jill noted that Crawford and Currey were taking notes as she spoke with Greenwood, who nodded at Jill's comment. "I understand you've got additional training in toxicology, so you likely know more about arsenic than we do."

"Yeah, I am board certified in toxicology. Which is a way of saying I've had additional training in the topic and have passed a test. Arsenic is an old poison dating back 3000BC. As it is odorless and tasteless, it's been a favorite poison to use for quite some time. Given the coarseness you described in the water filter, I'm thinking our suspect has some training in the sciences to understand that aspect. I would also bet that he or she practiced and tested to make sure they got the outcome they desired. In fact, one of the things my team is looking at is other deaths in trailer parks—especially trailer parks that are scheduled for closure."

"I thought you were done with this case as we've declared it a homicide," Crawford said.

"No. I took this case on pro-bono, as did my team. We all feel bad for Catherine's loss of her best friend and were mad that someone made Mary's life a misery before she passed. So, we'll stay on the case until it is solved."

"What if you can't solve it in the next month? Are you planning on staying on the case for five years or more if it goes cold?" Greenwood asked, looking skeptically at Jill. Crawford and Currey were giving her a look that said, "amateur."

"Look, I've been providing second opinions on the cause of the death for seven years now. In all that time, I haven't failed to solve a case in less than a month, and in fact most of my cases have been solved within two weeks. My team members bring unique and timely skills to an investigation. My home lab can run tests that sometimes can take your crime lab weeks to get results due to backlogs. My teammate Jo is a CPA and she has the nose of a blood hound for spotting financial issues that lead to murder—how long does it take your department to find a forensic accountant? Another teammate, Marie, is a social media maven who can create a dossier faster and better than the CIA. I have another friend whom I sometimes bring in on cases who is a computer whiz—he can out-compute Bill Gates. Finally, my last teammate has interview and photography skills that would do your department proud. So like it or not, we'll continue to look for evidence in this case to serve Mary Niles who died before she should have and her best friend who must now move to a new community without her. We will, of course, continue to share our findings with you, Detective."

That explanation wiped the superior expressions off the faces of Crawford and Currey. After a moment of silence, Greenwood said, "We have a retired detective working on our cold cases. She has assistance from a secret computer genius, and they have solved some amazing cases including reuniting a missing five-year-old with her parents. So I can't knock using citizen resources if they help us solve this case. The fact that you've said you'll share everything with us, and clearly you understand that you don't have arrest or interrogation powers, means we will get along well."

Jill nodded and continued her discussion of the evidence. "I asked Catherine Dobson to have her blood tested for arsenic as the two women drank tea together every morning. She gave me permission to share her personal medical information with law enforcement."

"Wouldn't boiling water for tea make the arsenic disappear?" Crawford asked.

"No. It's an element, so it doesn't evaporate. Boiling water makes it more concentrated, and you end up with less water than you started with. Catherine's blood showed a higher level of arsenic, but not yet dangerous to her. It should go back to normal in time. She had a cup of tea made from boiling water out of Mary's faucet. Mary didn't like to cook, so Catherine thankfully had no other opportunity to consume Mary's water."

"That's good news for Catherine," Greenwood said.

"Yes. Indeed."

"So what is your focus for solving this case?" Currey asked. He seemed genuinely curious to see what a lay person like Jill would focus on.

"We're looking at the investor whom Mary fought in court for nearly five years. We're also looking at other community members from their trailer park. We will also survey who outside of the trailer park has cameras that focus on the traffic going in and out."

"How about Catherine Dobson? Maybe she was mad at her best friend Mary over the court cases or something else. Perhaps she's our murderer," Greenwood said.

"I'll look into her as that is routine for me, but I don't think Catherine is our killer. I was called in on a case in Dallas by the murderer. When he saw me getting too close to the truth, I was fired. Fortunately, the police saw my value and hired me on. Interestingly, that was also a case of arsenic. Unlike this case, the spouse killed the wife with a blueberry muffin overdosed with arsenic, so she died quickly."

Jill continued, "With Mary's death, her murder was already covered up, so why would she call me into the case? Also, I doubt she has the physical strength in her hands to put that filter in line with the water. Finally, why would she choose a murder method that had the potential to make herself sick?"

During her explanation she saw nods of agreement at various points. She ended with a question for them, "Is there anything you're looking into that I missed or, given the resources at my fingertips, is there any piece of evidence you would like examined by my team?"

The three law enforcement representatives shook their heads, "No." Jill stood up to leave wondering if that was a truthful answer or just law enforcement's usual reticence with sharing information with a civilian. She had lots of research ahead of her and she also had her wine business to attend to. Her Moscato vintage sold out each year; however, her new red wine vintage had another one hundred cases or so to sell. She would visit a few more wine merchants and grocery stores located in her town. They were usually pretty good at purchasing local vineyards' wines.

"One final question—can you give me the name of the

manufacturer of the water filter?" Jill asked as she was about to exit the conference room. Greenwood sighed as looked through a folder, pulling out a piece of paper. It was from the crime lab and it contained a picture and manufacturer information. Jill took a picture of it with her cell phone. She thanked the detective and left.

She thought about wine distribution during her drive back home. She had plans for a tasting room, but with only two vintages, it was too soon to begin construction. She thought about creating an online store to sell direct, but she had a small member list that received announcements about the availability of new vintages, and no wine club was established yet. She would talk over her options with Nathan as he was due back this evening from his teaching gig at a renowned California wine university.

She returned to thinking about the case and mobile home parks. There was a mobile home park in a nearby city. She didn't often go by that area, but now she would check it out. Maybe talk to some of the residents about the ins and outs of such housing. She arrived at the location to find no mobile homes in the location. Maybe she had the wrong address. She pulled up Google Earth and no, she had the right location, it was just sometime between when the satellite picture was taken and now, the entire park disappeared. Why? What happened? She went to the county property records to see who owned the land.

The owner was HBZ Builders—the same company that was taking over Mary and Catherine's mobile home park community. The locations were about two hundred miles apart, yet the same devastation occurred in both communities. She wondered how much the investor paid the owners for the loss of their mobile home in this former park. That was another thing to add to her list of things to look up. She put her car in gear and headed home with lots of mental notes of things to research.

CHAPTER 8

*J*ill had disappeared down the rabbit hole when she heard Trixie run over to the door a moment before Nathan walked in carrying a backpack he used for classes. He dropped the backpack and overnight bag and walked over to where she was working to give her a kiss.

"How did your lectures go?"

"I think I've mentioned before that I can tell who has a future in marketing and who simply lacks the imagination. I think that every vineyard owner should take my class so if they hire out the marketing component of their winery, they'll be able to judge the work of someone else. As the instructor, I'm aware that I'm talking to two different groups of future vineyard workers. I find myself trying to directly talk to each group. Some days it's hard to find the words that will take an imaginative person to the next level of artistry and teach that other group how to expect more artistry. I imagine this will be a lifelong pursuit of how to reach both groups."

"I sense that you're enjoying the challenge of teaching both groups," Jill said.

"I am. There's another professor who teaches marketing and

his goal is for everyone to be an artist. I have to imagine that his students are frustrated that they can't meet his demands for vision. I've heard rumblings from my students about him."

"How did you solve the problem of engaging both groups?"

"I asked them to self-select at the start of the class as to whether they wanted to be the artist or to hire out that function for their future winery. I then paired them up. That way the artist learns how to listen to the customer and the non-artist learns how to express what they want to the artist. Then the team competes for a project grade. I change the team up for every project, so they all get the feel of working with different people."

"I imagine you come across 'artist students' who learn that they don't have a future as an artist."

"Sadly, yes. Many more students find out they're not graphic artists. I don't downgrade images in my grading scheme; rather, the team has to explain what their vision was and why their images met that vision. If they have a good reason for putting a poorly drawn sun on a label, it doesn't affect their grade if the sun was part of their vision. However, when we share and talk through projects in the class, it's obvious to all who has graphics artistry."

"Was that hard to learn to separate your grading on a lack of vision versus a lack of artistry?"

"Initially, yes. But I learned quickly. You can't make someone an artist who doesn't have that skill, but if you don't have the ability to draw competent graphics, then you at least had better know what the purpose of your graphics was. That's basically the point I'm driving home to my students all semester long."

"If I could be an invisible fly on the wall, I'd love to stop by your classroom and watch you work your magic with students and what you're trying to teach them."

"Actually, you could watch the end result of my teaching. I'm hosting my first end of semester forum and I've invited wineries looking for marketing help to view student projects and get their information if there's interest. The students haven't graduated yet, but it's a great way to dip their toes in the future industry, and the industry can get help without making a full-time commitment to someone. Some of the bigger wineries may be looking to supplement their marketing staff with someone exactly like my students. So it's a win—win."

"I would like to watch that; give me the date and I'll put it on my calendar. As I was driving home, I was thinking about my winery. I'm limiting myself because I have only two varietals at this time. I think I'll make a decision by the end of this week on additional varietals that I'll produce. I can plant now and harvest in five years, and in the interim buy grape juice to start experimenting and then producing those five new varietals now. If I buy juice now, I think I could have another couple of wines for sale in a few months. Once I have a production date for the new wines, I can work on building my tasting room."

"Wow, you decided all that while you were driving home?" Nathan asked.

"It was a result of my meeting with a San Francisco wine seller. He ordered 10 cases of my Nero d'Avola. So this week, I've sold about 20 cases of the 125 that I expect to have. I thought about how I would ship my product to the various merchants. Then I thought about how I was going to sell another 100 cases. It would be easier if I had a tasting room to sell direct. I do sell some of my wines online, but that's mostly dribs and drabs. However, in order for a tasting room to make sense, I need more than two wine varietals. Thus, the origin of my thoughts."

"Well, I'll be anxious to see what varietals you pick. The good news is you have fallow land ready to be planted as soon as you decide on the grape varietal."

"Any recommendations from a marketing perspective on what to plant?"

"I would do you a disservice by recommending a particular varietal. You're the winemaker—you're the one who needs to have the taste buds to recognize when a wine is perfect. I know you don't like dry wines, so obviously stay away from those. I might take another look at Sicily as we have similar climates. I'm excited to watch you grow your business and I can't wait to create your wine labels."

Jill gave Nathan a long hug. What more could she want in a partner? He didn't tell her she was crazy for wanting to expand her business. Instead, he provided light advice and support. She was so lucky in her choice of husband.

They moved on to dinner and other topics of conversation. Then he asked about her latest case.

"I visited the SJPD after the wine merchant in San Francisco. Mary Niles' death is officially a homicide—their medical examiner verified most of my findings. It takes longer for them to get test results back, as you know from other cases."

"Were they respectful?" Nathan asked hesitantly. He had seen the variety of emotions directed toward Jill over the years. Some law enforcement representatives were cooperative, and others had a spectrum of behavior from sarcastic to rude to disrespectful. Despite the fact that his wife had built a worldwide reputation as a sleuth, it seemed like she was forced back to square one with many cases.

"The lead detective had more brains than her two associates —a second detective and a criminalist from the D.A.'s crime lab. So it wasn't too bad until I told them I would be staying on the case."

Nathan grinned and replied, "They don't know you very well, do they? What happened?"

"I told them I had a duty to the victim and her best friend. I also listed Jo, Angela, and Marie's skills for them and taunted them with the fact that I've never not solved a case in less than a month. I doubt they'll share information with me going forward, but I'll share my findings with them."

"How was your victim poisoned?"

"That was ingenious. The killer took a typical charcoal filter, removed the charcoal, and replaced it with arsenic. He or she put it in line after her water connection so that every time Mary drank tea or made food, she ingested arsenic. It took probably six weeks to kill her."

"That's sad. So who is on your killer list?"

"Someone not yet identified—the investor company which is HBX builders, or maybe someone from the mobile home park. Mary fought the sale of the park for five years. In that time, she upset the builder and some of the community residents. While she didn't succeed in blocking the sale, she did get the reimbursement for their trailers and inconvenience of moving pushed higher."

"That sounds sad, pushing eighty-year-olds out of what they thought to be their forever homes."

"It is sad. I went by that trailer park off Highway 70 near the town of Linda as I thought about interviewing residents there about all things mobile home park wise and would you believe it's gone?"

"I HAVEN'T DRIVEN that way in a long while, but I remember the mobile home park you're talking about—it always seemed lively and full of people.

"Yes, very sad. I researched who bought it and it was the same investor company—HBX Builders. I'm really starting to dislike this company, and I know little about them."

"I'm going to take about an hour to get dinner ready. Why don't you talk with your friends about the case, and I'll interrupt you when it's ready."

"I love a man who takes charge in the kitchen. Thank you for cooking," Jill said as she leaned in to kiss him.

Jill walked over to her computer station and spent some time looking at the emails from Jo, Angela, and Marie.

Angela had taken the initiative and called about six or seven current and former mobile home park residents after reaching out to Catherine Dobson. It was an interesting group. Most liked their homes and their community. They were unhappy that they were pushed out. One of the residents said that while all home prices were increasing, mobile homes prices were not keeping pace. So, once they were forced out of their existing park, they would have to move to a cheaper city to afford another mobile home or else stay and rent. Angela was also able to collect the names of a few other people who died in their mobile home park. The names came up in conversations as apparently that was the source of a mobile home being available to buy.

Jill felt bad for these people losing their homes. It was an example of gentrification where the poorer neighbors get left behind. This was interesting and sad, but she didn't think it was a motive for murder.

Marie examined Mary and Catherine's social media presence. It wasn't that large given their age. There weren't that many eighty-five-year-olds who richly documented their lives on social media. The two ladies had taken a class and practiced posting but gave it up as they thought it was pointless. Marie was short on time and would research the investor company the next day. Jill sent Marie the names of Mary's unhappy neighbors to see if she found any problems with them.

She moved on to Jo's email which focused on the mobile home community and HBX Builders. Her early research suggested that the communities were privately managed. They were like a homeowners' association, and their finances were only revealed when properties were sold. Jo was thinking about asking for their friend Henrik's help with hacking into a few of the communities bought by HBX Builders or even the company itself.

As for the investing company, they were privately owned but were getting to the size where there was talk about taking the company public. That had resulted in a few more documents that Jo could examine than would normally be the case with a private company. They had a singular focus on mobile home parks sitting on expensive land. For the past decade, nearly all of their projects were conversions of mobile home parks to single-family homes or townhouse communities.

Jill researched statistics for mobile home parks in California. There were more than 5,900 parks for mobile homes and recreational vehicles. Some of those locations didn't cater to full-time non-recreational vehicle homes, and only 174 were parks where the mobile homeowner also owned the land beneath the trailer. That meant HBX had many mobile home parks they could take over. Granted, some of those parks were in cities that weren't targets for gentrification. That's what happened when the land beneath the park was worth so much more than the park landowner was making on rent for the land beneath the homes.

Jill took notes as she read her friends' emails on things she wanted to follow up on. She was startled that an hour had gone by, and Nathan interrupted her thinking with the announcement that dinner was ready.

"Do you have plans for this weekend? I thought we might take a trip somewhere for a long weekend. I know you're working on this recent murder, but it appears most of your work is by computer, so you don't need to be close to San Jose."

Jill smiled. This was one of the things she loved about Nathan—he understood how important her sleuthing work was to her. "You're right. I can do that from anywhere. Where were you thinking of going?"

"Not far, just to Paso Robles. They have a similar climate to here, so you could explore wine varietals there to potentially help you decide where to expand your offerings."

Jill leaned over to hug Nathan. He got her, and she was so lucky.

"That sounds like an excellent plan. Did you cook that up while you were fixing dinner?"

"I did. I checked a few places we could stay, and I checked with our house sitter to make sure we're covered with the pets. When does your bottling service arrive?"

"Next Tuesday, so we're good on that commitment too. Why don't you make all the arrangements you like, and I'll be along for the ride."

CHAPTER 9

Jill started out the morning finishing her research on the wine varietals. She needed grapes that liked her climate, and she preferred a varietal that was less common than her Moscato or a Cabernet Sauvignon. She thought about making Port as it was something she loved. However, she had been to Oporto, Portugal, and toured the Douro Valley. The United States was the last country that was labeling wines as "Port" even though the grapes weren't grown in Portugal. She was a purist and it seemed wrong to steal the name from Portugal.

She narrowed her grapes down to Barbera, Petit Verdot, Marsala, Sangiovese, and Syrah. The last two were far more common than the first three, and if the going got tough, she could always do a red blend. She copied Nathan on her list as he would set up a tour of the Paso Robles area that would feature tastings of those wines. The area had over two hundred wineries, so it wouldn't be hard to find those varietals. She liked these five wines, but now she needed to prove to herself that she had the skill to make a great wine with those grapes.

She moved back to the case of Mary Niles. She wanted to

start with the names of the three people that Angela provided who had passed away in a mobile home park before Mary's death. She searched the local funeral homes for details and found that all of them had been cremated. In some ways that was no surprise. The price of land in the region was expensive whether you were dead or alive. Funerals might cost $30,000 to $40,000 by the time all the arrangements were made, including the cost of a cemetery plot. A quick glance of cemetery plots for sale in San Jose had burial plots going from $5,000 to $25,000. Generally, people who lived in mobile home parks were lower income, so the only way to afford burial services was through cremation. For Jill, that meant that down the road if she wanted to exhume bodies, she was out of luck as all that was left was ashes. Even if the ashes were still available, there were no quantifiable tests that said this was the expected normal level of arsenic in them, or this level was high. Then, once the case got to court, there was no way to prove that the cremation process was pure—not a single ash from someone else's remains was not accidentally left behind for the next cremation.

She asked Marie to investigate the three residents on social media; maybe they had said something about not feeling well. She was unable to get into their medical records as she was not in a position of authority, and she was sure the police also couldn't get a subpoena for the records as they didn't have enough evidence for probable cause.

Jill decided to do a little research into the nearby mobile home park. When had it been demolished? When would construction start? If I were a resident pushed out of a home I loved, I would be mad if that land stood vacant for months to years, she thought. She took a moment to try to remember when she'd last driven by that park and realized it might have been at least a year. After a little search, she found it had been demolished three years ago. That was a long time for the land to sit idle. Then she thought of the next question—did HBX

Builders always keep mobile home parks for themselves or did they turn around and sell the land to another company? She would send that question to Jo.

She leaned back to think about the case. What other clues could she follow? What about the murder weapon, arsenic? Arsenic is an element found in the air, water, and soil. How did the killer figure out the water filter device to deliver the poison to Mary?

As usual, the first thing she did was search for a source of arsenic. There were many retailers for a homeopathic remedy called Arsenicum Album. It was used for a variety of gastrointestinal disorders. Upon further study, the manufacturing process eliminated most of the arsenic in the product. She could purchase arsenic crystals from a variety of sources and grind them into a powder to place inside the filter. She had no means of determining who purchased arsenic crystals. There were many sources that sold arsenic powder as it was used in industrial process and well as for calibration of analyzers.

Next, she researched the filter. She'd taken a picture of it and got the manufacturer's name from Detective Greenwood. This wasn't your average water filter as it wasn't the pressure of the kitchen sink faucet. Rather, this filter had to stand up to the pressure from the water company intake valve. Water companies could pump at rates as high as 120psi, but generally were in the range of 60—80psi. Kitchen sinks typically had pressure at 40—60 psi. Once you got beyond 60 psi, your water pressure started to affect appliances. Given that everything seemed a little more fragile with a mobile home, she wondered if they had a need for further reductions in psi. She dropped Catherine a question about appliances. It had nothing to do with the case at this point, but some days she just needed new knowledge for the sake of answering a question for her brain.

She took a break from the case and took Trixie for a run. On her way back, she stopped to look at her land and ruminate about where she would plant additional crops. She basically needed an acre to produce one thousand bottles of wine. She had more than five acres that she hadn't planted anything on. If she went with the five varietals she'd picked earlier, she would need to understand their growing peculiarities to see which acre would plant which grape. Some grapes liked steep land while others did fine on flat land. She had both topographies in her acreage and would be able to accommodate the grapes' growing preferences.

She returned home to find Nathan nursing his first cup of coffee. She waited to talk to him until he spoke to her. One of the rules of marriage—don't bombard Nathan with conversation until he engaged first—and it quietly amused her to follow this rule. To be fair, Nathan likewise understood not to engage Jill's brain after nine at night as her brain cells were likely running out of gas.

She walked over to her computer and planned to read her email while she waited for Nathan to speak. She looked at her watch and figured she had half an hour before he would be up to conversing and, in the meanwhile, she would try a search of all deaths in California in mobile home parks. A few minutes later, she gave up. There was simply no publicly reported state database that she could search for the answer. She then tried to search obituaries, but those announcements did not include street addresses, so it was a hopeless search. She sighed and leaned back. She decided she was looking for information in too big a pool.

What if she tried Angela's method? She'd found the names of mobile home park residents by asking other residents. Of course, why did she even care about other mobile home residents who died before their time? It was a weird niche for a serial killer to be at the source of premature deaths. However, what if this was an assassin? Hired by someone to kill a targeted number of people. Then she thought, "Oh come on, Jill, your imagination is wild this morning."

"I read your email on the wine varietals," Nathan said. "I'll plan our Paso Robles wine tastings with those in mind."

"Thank you. Do you have any comments on my choices?"

"Not really. I don't know much about the growing end of the wine business. You picked rarer varietals that someone generally won't ask for by name in a liquor store. Still, from a marketing perspective, if you want to stand out it will be easier with these choices. Imagine deciding to add Cabernet grapes; you be the five-thousandth producer and would compete against everyone else. Why would a wine seller sell your Cab versus someone else's bottle?"

"I picked these grapes based on whether I think I like their flavors. You know, if it is a dry grape, I would have a hard time trying to make a good vintage as it all tastes bad to me."

"Don't ever admit to a wine judge or a customer that you can't stand dry wines. Wine makers are supposed to love all grapes equally," Nathan said with a smile. "What are you working on today?"

"I need to sell a few more cases of wine. I also want to talk to some mobile home residents. How about you?"

"I've got to plan our weekend. I'm working on materials for several clients, and I have a few emails to contend with regarding the university. Just an average day. Speaking of which, I need to head over to my studio."

Jill nodded, it did indeed sound like an average day for the two of them. Ten minutes later he was gone. When they married, Nathan moved into her house as she needed to be near her grapevines and labs. He drove to his studio situated near his old house. He hadn't decided what to do with the house. His studio and house were on the same piece of land. He could rent out the house, divide the parcel and sell the house, or move his studio and sell the entire lot. He thought about building a studio on Jill's land as she had an area that she didn't intend to use to plant grapevines or build her tasting room on. He could walk to work; granted it was a two-mile hike. Jill's land was more out of the way to the town they lived in, but his clients came from all over the state and even out of state, so a ten-mile move wasn't going to change his cliental.

CHAPTER 10

Jill thought about working outside, but it had rained overnight and likely was muddy. She decided to stay inside and think about Mary's killer some more. They were smart, as they picked a method and a target that was unlikely to be noticed. If not for her good friend, Catherine, Mary's murder would have gone unrecognized. The killer also found the source of arsenic and the right filter to place in line to the water supply. They likely had fake identification labeling themselves as a water company employee and knew how to insert the filter without having a plumbing disaster. Mary might have even met her killer.

Could there be a second killer? Did Mary's killer have help? Was this a one and done murder, or was the motive such that there would be more victims out there? If there was more than one victim, did the killer use the same method?

According to FBI stats, nearly half of all murders were one killer and one victim. More than three quarters were male victims and nearly three quarters were killed with a gun. So on many statistical levels, Mary's murder was unusual.

She looked at the time and thought her friends might have

answers soon as their time zone was two hours ahead. She received an email from Catherine answering her question about appliances. Mary's washing machine and refrigerator ice maker had both gone on the blink about three weeks prior. It frustrated Mary as they were so close to having to abandon their mobile homes. That suggested that the filter had caused higher water pressure in her home. Interesting, but not a fact that helped solve Mary's murder. However, it was telling on the timing of when the filter was put in line to her water supply.

How about cameras in the area? Was there any chance that someone had cameras that may have caught the fake water company vehicle on camera? So many cameras held footage for only thirty days, and this filter might have been in place as much as forty-five days ago based on Mary's onset of symptoms. Then she thought of another idea—she should go to the mobile home park and see if that filter was on any of the other water connections to the trailers. Furthermore, she should find some additional trailer parks that were in the process of being sold or were recently sold to HBX Builders and see if she could find the filter on any other trailers. It wasn't that anything hinted of a serial killer; however, it was a fairly sophisticated murder weapon, and she didn't think it was a one and done murder.

With that idea in mind, she looked up additional mobile home parks related to HBX Builders and then made the drive toward Mary's mobile home park. She had the cameras and the filter to investigate as a routine question into the death of Mary Niles. She should have thought of it when the first filter was discovered. Perhaps even now other residents were being poisoned. Maybe law enforcement thought of this already and did a search. Catherine's house was the only house deemed safe from arsenic in that community. As she drove, she thought about locations to sell her wine, making mental notes to herself to follow up.

She reached Catherine's neighborhood and parked a good block away. As she walked toward the community, she looked around for door cameras as well as those at intersections. She took down addresses that had door cameras. Then she began walking around the mobile home park. It had a very sad look about it as about half of the homes already had been abandoned. There were about 110 or so mobile homes. She was given a suspicious look by one of the residents. If they knew that Mary had been murdered then she understood the resident's concern. She called Catherine to see if she was available to walk with her. That would allay the concerns of any of the residents.

"Hi Catherine, I'm here in your mobile home park looking for additional water valves that shouldn't be there and I'm getting suspicious looks. I wondered if you could walk with me so that people don't end up calling the police on me?"

"Of course I can do that. Where are you in the park?"

"I'm by the pool."

"Be there soon."

Jill leaned against the fence surrounding the pool and again looked for doorbell cameras or carport cameras, but the only cameras she saw were on homes that likely were abandoned which meant there was no feed for them. A few minutes later she saw Catherine walking toward her. While she said her friend Mary was in excellent shape, she noticed that Catherine was walking without an aid like a cane. She also was in good shape.

"Catherine, thanks for coming over at the last minute. I need to compliment you on your fitness. You're walking without help, so you must be staying in shape somehow. You bragged about Mary being in shape, but you're doing well also."

"Thank you. I do try and walk several miles a day. We used to have fitness classes here, but that went away once residents started leaving. It was one of the things I looked for in my next community. So you're here looking for more water valves like the one at Mary's house?"

"I am. I got thinking that we looked at your house, but I didn't look at any other houses and I thought I heard that other residents had passed away. I seem to have run out of clues to follow, but I've been giving a lot of thought to the killer. They used such a sophisticated method of killing Mary that I don't think there's been only one death."

"Oh my."

"Yes. I have to think there are additional people who have been killed by this method. So have other residents been killed here or at another mobile home park? The builder that bought this community has a focus on mobile home communities and has bought several throughout the state. They even bought a park that is about twenty to thirty minutes from my home. It's sad as they forced the people to move, then demolished the trailers that were homes, and now the land is sitting vacant waiting for them to get around to building a new community."

"That is sad. You take people to court to take their land from them, and once you get it you don't do anything with it even though you've upended the lives of people living there," Catherine said.

"Yes," Jill agreed as they walked by trailers looking at the water connections. "Do you remember if anyone else has passed away in this community that you were surprised about?"

There was silence as they reached the end of one street and started to follow the next street. Catherine pointed at a trailer that looked unoccupied.

"Mr. Bishop lived in this trailer. He passed perhaps eight months ago. He seemed in good health and was in his 70s I would guess. It seemed like from one day to the next he was well and then he died. His wife died perhaps a decade ago and they had no children. His niece checked on him and included him in family dinners on major holidays. I think it was around

Easter when she hadn't heard from him for a few days and drove over to his home. She found him dead. I think the police investigated, but decided he died from natural causes."

"Is that another arsenic valve?" Catherine asked, pointing at the water pipes.

"It sure looks like one. Let me alert Detective Greenwood and we'll continue our search." Jill called the detective, but she didn't pick up, so she left a voicemail with what they found. "Let's continue our search. Hopefully, that's the only valve we find. Has anyone else died here in the past year that you remember?"

Jill could tell Catherine was thinking about her neighbors and they passed three more homes before she answered.

"We had another death due to cancer and one due to heart disease."

"Had they been sick for a while or is that what the family said was the cause of their death?"

"The one resident was undergoing chemo, the other I didn't know well enough to guess."

"Have we examined those two houses yet?"

"Yes, and they had no filter."

"Okay. Then hopefully we won't find any more filters. Was the other victim fighting the sale of the community?"

"Yes. Once he passed, Mary became the leader to fight the sale."

They continued down the street and finished looking at all the houses. The remainder of the houses were clear. They started walking back to Catherine's home, when an unmarked car pulled into the community. The window was down, and Jill could see Detective Greenwood. Good, the authorities had arrived.

"You found another arsenic filter?"

"Yes, follow us," Jill said, proceeding down the street. She stopped at the abandoned home and waited for the detective to exit her car. Detective Crawford got out of the car and the two of them followed Jill and Catherine. They stood back as the detectives examined the pipe.

"Let's get the water company out here to examine this pipe. Did you look at every mobile home in this park?" Greenwood asked.

"Yes. This is the only one. Catherine said the occupant was found dead by his niece, but no autopsy was performed that she was aware of. I looked for his obituary to see if he was cremated, but I didn't find anything yet."

"I'll find out," Crawford said, stepping away from them.

"How are you doing, Catherine? Are you tired from being on your feet taking me around the park?" Jill asked.

"It's not so much that I'm tired. I'm sad that some loon is out there picking on old people."

Jill rubbed Catherine's shoulder. She had seen the worst of people in her career both as a medical examiner and as a private investigator.

Crawford came back and said, "Greg Bishop is buried in a local cemetery. I'll contact his niece to see about getting his remains exhumed. Dr. Quint, will arsenic still be in his remains?"

"There should be a higher level of arsenic in the remains, but what will be telling is a look at the organs most affected by arsenic—kidneys, liver, and heart."

"We'll see what our medical examiner finds. Do you think there are other deaths out there? What made you look at this mobile home park?" Greenwood asked.

"I thought the method of murder was sophisticated. Most people who die by intentional arsenic poisoning do so because their food was poisoned. These water valves took some science on the part of the killer as well as patience for the death to occur. Besides, who would randomly target Mary Niles? I thought there had to be more. HBX Builders has a decades-long record of buying mobile home parks and turning them into upscale homes. They've been so successful at this strategy that they're considering taking the company public."

"Wait, are you accusing a company of these murders, Dr. Quint? That seems very far-fetched and nothing that I've heard of in my twenty years as a detective," Greenwood said.

"It's not a company planning a murder; rather, they're clearing obstacles to making more money. The motive is greed, one of the oldest motives known to mankind."

"Huh," Greenwood said with a skeptical expression on her face.

"I just had a conversation with Mr. Bishop's niece. She's still grieving his death, and she's thrilled we want to exhume his remains. I'm going to head back to the office to write this up and get a judge to approve the order. I've got a squad car stopping by to give me a ride," Crawford said.

Greenwood nodded and said, "I'm waiting for the water company and Currey to arrive to collect evidence."

"Detective, I have an incomplete list of mobile home parks that HBX Builders have purchased in California over the last five years or so. Despite payouts to mobile home tenants, it's been a very lucrative practice. My accounting expert says there are two types of mobile home parks—one where you own the land beneath your home and another where you pay rent on that land. HBX builders has been able to purchase those mobile home parks where the land is rented much faster than parks like this one where they own the land as well as the home. What are your thoughts about a motive for Mary Niles' death?"

"I don't have a motive yet," Greenwood said.

"Well, I've been puzzling about it. It's a science-based murder. It took a whole different level of planning than your average homicide. I can't imagine how an 85-year-old woman without heirs might inspire an as-yet-unknown person to go to a lot of trouble to kill her. So that has left me searching for a motive to solve this homicide and wondering if this arsenic filter has been used on other residents. According to Catherine, Mr. Bishop was also quite the fighter against the sale of this community. There's also an arrogance level on the part of this killer as they haven't returned to remove the filter. It's like they're sure that they aren't going to be caught so they leave the murder weapon in plain sight."

Greenwood nodded but didn't say anything. This might be because they noticed a water department vehicle arriving or because she wasn't planning on sharing any information with Jill even though Jill felt like she was uncovering all the clues in this homicide.

It was the same set of water employees as were on scene earlier in the week. Catherine had entered the pool enclosure and was sitting on a chaise lounge. She was close enough to answer questions, but she was resting her feet. They walked over to the new meter and watched as the water company removed the valve and placed it in a paper bag that the detective held open.

"We're going to examine all of the water valves in this community, Detective. We've never seen anything like these valves being placed in line in a water system."

"Dr. Quint already examined the water lines and didn't find any other valves, but I welcome your examination," Greenwood said.

"Can you test that valve to see if you have arsenic in it? I forgot to bring my test kit," Jill asked.

"Sure."

A short time later they had their positive test for arsenic.

"Did your friends find any other communities in San Jose that are being sold to HBX Builders?" Greenwood asked Jill. "I'd like to send the water company over to one of them if that's the case."

Jill nodded, looking for the list that Jo had found in the financial filings for the company.

After a search of her email, she said, "There are two other communities and one is located near the fairgrounds; the other is near Eastridge Mall. Both of these purchases were in the last year, so hopefully some of the buildings are still there."

The detective pulled up a satellite image which showed the trailer parks as still there, but who knew when the image was taken? Satellite images could be upwards of three years old.

"Would you like to follow me over there, Dr. Quint?" Greenwood asked.

"Yes. Which location are you going to first?"

"Which location is the most recent purchase?"

Jill reviewed the email and said, "The park near Eastridge. Shall we head there?"

The detective nodded and Jill provided the address. Jill walked over to Catherine to say goodbye as well as tell her what they were up to, and soon entered her car to follow the detective. Jill figured that the detective didn't so much as want to include her as she wanted to have a second pair of eyes in her search.

CHAPTER 11

It was just past midday, so the traffic wasn't bad, and they were at the location in under twenty minutes. Jill sighed when they pulled up to the address. Much of it was already demolished. A few buildings remained, with a construction tractor at work. Detective Greenwood approached the operator of the tractor holding out her badge. Jill couldn't hear the conversation, but she heard the tractor engine being turned off, so they apparently got a reprieve to look at the mobile homes. As Jill walked inside the construction area, she noted some demolition garbage bins filled with stuff.

She walked over to the detective as she assessed the situation. "It looks like we have two areas to look at here. There are a few trailer homes still standing. It also looks like the demolition crew is sorting debris. I think that bin over there has pipes and other metal in it. How do you want to split the work?"

"I'll take the bin. I don't want to be responsible for any injury you incur looking through that bin," Greenwood said, looking at the jagged debris in the bin.

Jill was fine with that response as she hadn't looked forward to examining the refuse. She suspected the detective would have to get additional staff and perhaps equipment to search the contents of the bin. She walked over to the remaining six or so houses looking for water meters. She quickly discovered that none of these water flow devices were tampered with. So she walked over to the bin where the detective was working.

"Detective, all the houses were clear. Should I let the construction dude know he can continue with demolition as long as he doesn't dump pipes on you?"

"Yes, and stand outside so we're sure he doesn't accidentally drop debris in this container."

Jill followed the detective's instructions and stood outside the bin to make sure she stayed safe. She wondered if the detective would be covered in gross demolition dirt and grease when she was finished.

"Found it!" she yelled from the bin about twenty minutes later. She pitched a bent pipe out of the bin and onto the ground near Jill. Then she climbed out of the bin. At least she was wearing latex gloves so her hands inside were clean. Once she landed on the ground, she said, "Yuck!"

She took her gloves off and made a call explaining her results. They had no means of determining which house the pipe came from, but some resident probably died from arsenic poisoning before they had to move. More importantly, HBX Builders shot to the top of their list of suspects. They were going to have do some research about the former residents of this mobile home park. She wondered about the type of community—did they pay rent for the land underneath their home, or did they own the land?

While the detective was handing out instructions, she tried to figure out the answer to her question. Perhaps an old real estate listing mentioned the land arrangement. She pulled up a few real estate sites and searched for listings that were three to five years old. Jill found that both communities were old, and each mobile homeowner owned the land underneath their home. That meant that if the community was sold, nearly all the residents had to agree to it, or perhaps some ratio like 80 percent. Getting most or all the residents to agree on something was difficult.

The detective ended her calls and said to Jill, "You might be right that there is some connection to HBX Builders. I have a squad car going to the other mobile home park location near the fairgrounds. It's probably already demolished, but if it isn't we need to examine the site. However, at this moment I'm afraid to leave this bin unguarded. That guy running the demolition tractor could care less about saving any evidence. The department won't thank me for claiming an entire demolition bin, so I'm kind of stuck until the crime scene crew gets here."

"I can run over to the other location if your squad car says there is anything on the lot," Jill said. "Maybe we'll luck out with another demolition bin, though I doubt it. I would think HBX Builders would be quick to clear the property if only for liability reasons and fear of squatters taking over, so my money is on an empty lot or an empty lot with construction underway for a new community and no sign of the mobile homes."

"I couldn't believe when you first suggested the builder as a suspect, but this case is getting weird quickly. I don't suppose you have any nearby cities with mobile home parks that HBX has bought out?"

"I don't have an all-inclusive list, but I do have more locations throughout the state. I believe there are locations in both adjacent counties—Alameda and San Mateo."

"Let me process the evidence here, and you check on the other lot. Then, I'd like to meet with you to examine the data you have," Greenwood said.

"As you probably know, I don't live in the area. I'd like to beat it out of here before my commute time gets doubled. Why don't we set a meeting time around ten tomorrow and we'll discuss our findings?" Jill said, hoping the detective picked up on the word, *our* meaning she would share with Jill.

The detective seemed to think about her day and her evidence collection and nodded.

"In fact, I'll leave for home now but drive by the other mobile home park on my way out of town just in case the squad car finds something. That way you can concentrate on this site today."

"You've been more helpful than I expected from a private citizen. Thank you. If not for you, this potential serial killer would have gone unnoticed."

Jill nodded and said, "You're welcome. See you tomorrow," and headed for her car. She put the GPS coordinates in the map app and followed it to the other mobile home park location.

A police squad car was parked at the curb of the demolished mobile home park. There was a cyclone fence around the property and one dumpster sitting inside. Jill parked her car and went over to the squad car.

"Hello, officers. I'm Dr. Jill Quint and I'm working with Detective Greenwood on this case. Here's her cell phone number if you would like to verify that," Jill said, handing over a piece of paper. They probably knew her number, but the SJPD had over one thousand officers, so it was conceivable that they didn't know the detective.

"Just a moment, ma'am."

She stepped away from the car as an officer made the phone call. She walked over to the tarp-covered cyclone fence to look through the breaks in the tarp. She spotted a dumpster on the property. The fence was locked with a length of chain and a padlock.

The officer stepped out of their car and walked over to Jill.

She used her cell phone to take a picture of the dumpster and texted it to the detective. Given that the gate was locked, and it was private property, the police would need a search warrant to get into the dumpster. Then she had a thought. She owned a drone, but it was home in Paradise Valley. The police also had drones and likely could use one to look into the dumpster.

She called the detective to relay her idea. "Detective, it occurs to me that your department could bring in a drone to see what's in that dumpster and whether it's worth your effort to get a search warrant to examine it closer. It's just a suggestion on my part."

"That's an excellent idea. Let me work on that."

The officers had been able to hear her side of the conversation, so after she ended the call, she said, "The detective is going to get somebody here with a drone to see if there's any possibility that she needs a search warrant for this property. On the odd chance that the dumpster is scheduled for pickup today, I suppose you guys should stay here until your department arrives with that drone to make sure the dumpster doesn't disappear. You might check with the detective."

Jill soon departed for the drive home. She had lots of thoughts in her head of what she needed to follow up on. She made a note to follow up with her friend, an IT wizard, Henrik Klein, to see if he might find old satellite images of the property or of the demolition. That was a long shot. However, if there was another resident in this location who died before their time according to relatives and was buried in a local cemetery, the detective might be able to locate another victim. Yes, they wouldn't have the murder weapon, but it was more about the pattern here. Jill dictated her thoughts into her phone as she drove, so she wouldn't forget anything. This case was becoming more troubling as it expanded from the untimely death of an eighty-five-year-old to multiple arsenic deaths.

Traffic was starting to build, and her commute home took longer than expected. She arrived home needing to stretch her legs and ponder the relative simplicity of being a vineyard farmer. She and Trixie strolled through the rows of dormant vines and the dog chased off a few squirrels. After half an hour, she felt refreshed and ready to plunge back into this complicated case.

Jill sat at her computer staring at the screen and trying to prioritize what to do first. She decided to read any emails from her friends as that might add to her list or re-prioritize the tasks. Then she had a thought about having Marie or Angela investigate the mobile home parks in counties nearby to San Jose. If there were multiple counties involved, then that would require the FBI to enter the case as the case was beyond one police jurisdiction. She decided Marie was the best at searching social media to find what people were saying about their park—especially a park that had been abandoned perhaps three years ago.

Jo emailed her a list of mobile home parks that HBX builders had purchased over the past five years. She provided standard information about the company, said they were doing well financially, and answered her question concerning whether they ever resold the land. They did that historically, but Jo's impression was they had improved their projection of which mobile home parks could bring them a projected ROI. Jo indicated that she really had nothing more to add to the case. Jill thanked her for her work and moved on to Angela, but she had nothing more to contribute as there was no one to interview.

Jill moved on to Marie's email. She was able to locate social media groups dedicated to each of the mobile home parks. There was also another app's website she checked that was devoted to neighborhoods. It was sad reading about the fight to block the sale, then the neighbors turning against one another, and then the sale being approved and people leaving a place they had known for over a decade. In many circumstances, the residents had to relocate to a new, cheaper city. This was not easy for anyone, but especially the older residents. Marie managed to tease out who were the most vocal opponents to each community's sale. In each case, the person died before they had to move according to the posts. What were the odds of the happening? Because she knew Jill would ask, she went a step farther to determine if they were cremated or buried. Gosh, she loved her friends—they anticipated what she would ask next and provided her with the answer even though they weren't being paid for their work. They had the same spirit as her with a desire to help people.

Jill now had a bunch of names to follow up on. Unfortunately, most of the mobile home park rabble rousers were cremated, so there was only one body to exhume, and it was a county in Central California. Now that Marie found the names, she looked up their old social media posts to see if there was any mention of not feeling well before their death. In some cases, there was a health issue and in others it was not mentioned. That could be because the person had no symptoms of arsenic poisoning before their death, or it might be that they didn't discuss such issues on social media.

Jill then had a thought: was HBX currently in the process of purchasing any mobile home parks? She went back to Jo's notes, and while she mentioned that buying the communities was their strategy, she didn't say which parks were under consideration. She wondered if she could do a social media search to locate any such parks.

Jill spent the remainder of the afternoon searching for the information, but she found no gossip. She would ask Marie to tackle that question for her as she had a feeling that her lack of answers was her internet searching technique and not a lack of information. She decided to set it aside and spend some time focused on Nathan. Maybe something would strike a flame in her brain for another clue to search if she focused on something else for a while.

CHAPTER 12

She pulled some chicken out of the freezer. She didn't like to cook, but sometimes she could make up her mind about what to have Nathan cook, and he appreciated not having to make that decision himself. She set the chicken in water to accelerate the defrosting. Then she went outside to stare at her grapevines. Her behavior likely looked dumb to a non-winemaker, but staring at her vines seem to help her with decision making regarding her wine business. She had plans for her tasting room and had the funds to build it, but she had to admit to herself that she was worried that no one would stop by to do the actual tastings, especially if she only had two varietals.

Still, her vineyard gave her peace. It brought her joy. She loved watching her grapes plump up, and her experiments with organic pest controls gave her much pleasure. She even liked hearing the leaves flutter when the grapes were long gone but the vines were still alive. Today, the vines looked dormant with no leaves or grapes, but she liked to think they were like the fat bears in Alaska. They soaked up the sun all summer to get as fat, juicy, and sweet as possible; then in the winter they slept while new growth occurred. Unlike the bears, though, she wasn't feeding them salmon.

She heard Nathan's car pull into the driveway and his door slam close. He had seen her on the edge of the vineyard when he arrived, and they walked toward each other. After a kiss of welcome, she mentioned that she'd pulled chicken out for him to cook, and he asked her how the case was going.

Nathan wasn't bored by her describing the details of any case. He frequently was amazed over the reasons for murder. They often were so petty. With this case, he worried about random seniors getting poisoned because they had stood up for themselves and fought against the sale of their home. He had parents in the age group of people being targeted in this case and he'd checked on his parents to make sure that no one was harassing them. She leaned against him as they both stared at her vineyard for a few moments.

Then she said, "If I plant the five new varietals, I'm going to have to hire more help. This is about all I can handle by myself. It's even worse if someone needs my services close to harvest season. I always shut down my second opinion on the cause of death service website so no one can find me and tempt me with an intriguing case."

"It is hard being dividing between two loves, and during harvest time, they both have very specific deadlines. It's not like you can say to a potential client, 'Ask the mortuary to put your loved one's remains in a freezer until I can get to it after I harvest my grapes.'"

"No, I can't say that to a family and even if I could, it would spoil the evidence I collect," Jill said. "Thanks for meeting me out here. I read the emails from my friends and then just needed to clear my head for a while. Glancing at the vines does that for me. Let's go inside and prepare dinner."

As they walked inside, Nathan asked a question he thought

he knew the answer to, "When will you retire from your consulting job?"

"I don't know. Perhaps when my friends stop helping me. I don't think I could solve most of these cases without their help. Besides, I enjoy working with them."

Nathan thought he knew his wife, but she had surprised him with that answer. He thought it would be beyond that point as she got so much satisfaction from solving these cases.

An hour later they were cleaning the dishes and planned to watch a movie together. There was a time when Jill wanted to do nothing except work all hours of all the day until a case was solved. Now she recognized that her brain was working in the background while she focused on something that had nothing to do with a murder case.

Fortunately, it was a shorter film—just under an hour and a half. As she expected, her brain was working on the problem, while her eyes were glued to the screen. Once it ended, Nathan planned to do some design work. She went over to her computer to ask Jo for information. She wanted to know who the board members and CEO were for HBX Builders. She could have looked it up herself, but she bet that Jo had the information at her fingertips. Who at HBX was killing people? Who had a science background to understand how to rig the murder weapon? She also needed another statistic—did every HBX Builders mobile home park have what seemed to be a premature death? Jill found herself rubbing her hands together thinking about the possibilities for research. Earlier in the day, she had felt like she was running out of clues to follow, but she was re-energized with new leads to pursue.

She started to fade as it had been a busy day. She kissed Nathan and headed upstairs to their bedroom; he'd be up in a few hours. It was odd that she did her best work before noon, while he did his best work after seven at night, and yet they were married with such diverse sleep schedules. She drifted off to sleep thinking about her mysterious murderer.

She awoke to an email from Detective Greenwood. Surprisingly, she was updating Jill on the case. It was rare that law enforcement voluntarily gave her information. The drone search of the garbage bin showed nothing, and they didn't think they had enough information to get a search warrant for the bin. The community was torn down over a year ago, so even if evidence was found there, they would have a hard time linking it to their criminal case as the garbage bin was unattended for that length of time. Also, the body of the other related person from Catherine Dobson's community was due to be exhumed today. Finally, the crime lab verified that the water valve contained an arsenic filter and was the same brand as the one at Mary's home. As the case was beginning to look like that of a serial killer, a call to the FBI would be made that day. The detective thought Jill might get a call from them as she was a key witness.

Little did the detective know that Jill had prior contacts with the FBI. Specifically, Leticia Ortiz, the Special Agent in Charge of the San Francisco office, had assisted her on a few cases. Jill debated calling Leticia, but figured she would get a call from the agent later that day. Even if another agent was responding to the case, Leticia would likely be informed. She planned to do more computer searches on the HBX Builders leadership team as well as follow up on the additional deaths. That way she would be prepared when the agent called. Marie had had time to follow up on more rabble rousers from other mobile home parks and sent Jill another email. It was awesome that Marie was an early riser and lived in a time zone two hours ahead of hers, so she generally got early morning answers.

Jill read through the email and determined that most parks had a few residents who were very antagonistic about the sale of the community. Not everyone died, though. From what she could see, no community had more than two very unexpected deaths. One community lost four people, but one was end-stage cancer and the other was a hard-smoking emphysema resident. Sure, arsenic could have pushed them on their way to an early death, but they were vocal in the beginning and then ran out of steam as the demands of their illness took over. Also, of note was that some of the parks were located in the states of Arizona and Nevada. She wondered if this would explode into a multi-state investigation. If it did, which seemed far-fetched, then they had a huge problem on their hands. She reminded herself to keep Catherine Dobson informed of the most recent details of the case. Perhaps it would in some way ease the grief she had been experiencing over the loss of her friend. It wouldn't bring Mary back to life, but the perp would be identified.

Jill took a break to make breakfast and was sitting down at her kitchen island when her phone rang. Yep, Leticia was on the case, according to her caller ID.

"Can't you stay out of trouble?" was the agent's opening question.

"You know I live to increase your workload, Special Agent," Jill said with humor in her voice.

"I'll say. We received the referral from the San Jose Police Department, and I've read through it. When your name was mentioned, one of my agents knew to route it to me. Tell me what you know."

"I took on this pro-bono case hoping to help the eighty-five-year-old best friend of the first identified victim. It's exploded into much more. I'm struck by the subtle and calculated murder weapon."

"Yeah, I recall you're a toxicologist in addition to being a pathologist. Tell me more about the murder weapon."

"Someone is using a carbon filter that is for the water line coming into a house. They take out the carbon and replace it with arsenic. There's some serious science there as well as the patience to wait for death to occur. It's likely taking four to six weeks. The killer had to figure out a filter that would withstand the pressure coming from the water main, and they needed to find a type of arsenic that would kill. They had to hope that their intended victim drank from the water supply. In at least two of the deaths, the victim felt bad for perhaps two to three weeks before their death and went to their doctor, but no one would routinely test for arsenic, so the cause wasn't found. In an autopsy, I routinely test for a variety of poisons and instantly found it. Then I had the neighbor who called me into the case get tested and she came back for arsenic, but not a fatal level. She and the victim drank tea together each morning. When I discovered those results, I brought a testing kit with me the next day to test the victim's water and it proved positive, so I called the water department and they discovered the filter, and then I called the SJPD."

"Is the victim's friend going to be okay?"

Jill liked that the agent was concerned about Catherine Dobson.

"Yes, it will wash out of her blood in a week or so, and she's not consuming more arsenic through Mary Niles' tap anymore."

"So," the Detective said, "this was linked to a company?"

"Yes. There's a California company named HBX Builders. Jo did some research on them and they're a private company contemplating going public, so there was a little more information than normal on a private company. Their strategy is to buy mobile home parks in California, Nevada, and Arizona, demolish the mobile home park, and replace it with luxury homes. The victim was in a park that was going through that process. She and another resident were the loudest opponents to this takeover."

"What happened to the other opponent?" Ortiz asked.

"We'll know later today or tomorrow. His body is being

exhumed and his family said he died before his time. The Santa Clara County ME will be examining the remains."

"Then there was another park?"

"Turns out there are a few more parks. Let me back up and say that mobile home parks have two models. One model is that you rent the space under your mobile home, and the other is you own the land. As you can imagine, it's much easier to force residents to go if they don't own their land. Here's my commentary—this is very shady. These are low-to middle-income residents, many of them up in years, and it's just mean-spirited to take the residents away from what they see as their forever home. I tell you this so you understand that I hate this company's strategy, and I'm biased to dislike them."

"Got it."

"Okay. Still, I find it hard to believe that a corporation is doing this. Surely it would take an executive either carrying out the action or paying someone else to do it. Jo guessed they made between half a million and a four million dollar profit depending on where the mobile home park was located."

"Killing someone for half million profit seems risky, especially when other projects can bring in four million. Then again, we have our fair share of murders that occur in the US for just one hundred thousand dollars—just look through our files. Heck, if you look at bank robberies, when someone accidentally get murdered, that amount is often less than ten thousand. However, this is a strange case. I'm having a hard time remembering a case where a corporation was the prime suspect."

"Exactly. Corporations do bad things all the time; but murder—how do you keep that plan quiet? How do you find murderous people to be in cahoots with? I don't doubt that you can find an assassin on the dark web, but still, these are little old ladies and men on low incomes in mobile home parks. How low are you to take these kinds of folks out? It's a head scratcher for me. Also, the only thing we have leading us to the corporation is the fact that they are the purchaser of these parks. That's almost no evidence and I'm sure a judge would laugh you out of his chamber."

"I actually wouldn't go to a judge with such little evidence for that very reason. So what else are you doing with this case?"

"Maybe I handed all my data and evidence over to Detective Greenwood and I'm not doing anything with the case," Jill suggested.

"Yeah, right. That's NOT the Jill Quint I know. What are you working on?"

"I'm looking in my backyard as well as Nevada and Arizona," Jill said.

"I know you said they were buying in Arizona and Nevada, but I thought this was just a California case."

"It may be, but the company has deployed these same tactics in those two states, so why wouldn't there be the same scenarios? I also want to look into a city about half an hour from me called Linda. There was a mobile home park there that has disappeared, and yet nothing is being built. It's owned by this company and the lot is sitting empty. If I were one of the residents forced out, I would be furious that I was made to move and then that land just sat there. Each of these mobile home residents has to leave the city they are in because of housing costs. They are low to low-middle income, and they get bought out for a fair market value, but nothing more. They have the cost of moving, they may have to find new doctors, they may be forced to move away from family, etc. Fair market value just isn't enough in this situation. That's the point that some of the protestors have made—they've pushed for more compensation. In some cases, they have gotten it, but I can't say that it's enough to cover their move."

"So maybe I can add elder abuse to whatever charges we come up with beyond murder."

"It would be nice to get back-compensation for all the residents who lived in all of these parks for the past five years. It's likely thousands of people. That would make me feel better. I can't reverse the deaths of people like Mary Niles, but money does help ease the situation for this group of people. Do you know that many of them choose cremation not because they want that, but because they can't afford any other service? I could go on and on about how I would like to see the right thing done with this group of people, but that won't help solve the case."

"I hear you. What do you think are the next steps?" Ortiz asked.

"First, we need to get results from the exhumation. That will tell us a lot about the case. If we have two at this one park, and we have suspicions about other parks based on Marie's and Angela's work, then we may have a serial killer or a serial assassin, though I'm not sure what the difference is between the two groups. Maybe you can get your behavior analysis unit involved to understand the psychology in this case."

"Tell me more about your colleagues' research."

"As you know Angela is best at face-to-face interviews, but she managed to talk to a few different residents with the help of Catherine Dobson. It was her impression that in each mobile home community dealing with this situation, there were one to three residents who would fight by using every legal angle to stop or delay or get a higher fair market value. Each resident was over, say, seventy and began to feel unwell and eventually slowed down their fight with the sale. Then they would die, and people would say, well they are old, and the local coroner or medical examiner would agree that the person died of old age. Which is never a true statement. You don't die of old age; you die because one of your organs gives out."

"Which organ gives out with arsenic poisoning?"

"Usually, it's the kidneys or liver."

"So how many mobile home communities are you actively looking at? I've lost track."

"Three in San Jose, one in Linda, and two others near San Jose, but out of the county. I haven't specifically looked at the situations in Nevada and Arizona, I just know I probably should."

"Got it. Let me talk to my sources here and organize a meeting later today, so stay available. This isn't a big grape growing season for you, is it?"

The special agent knew of Jill's other passion.

"Yes and no. There's nothing I need to actively do in the vineyard, but Nathan and I are running to Paso Robles this weekend and I have a bottling truck coming next Tuesday. So you have me today and maybe tomorrow morning. I'm adding five new varietals to my vineyard, and I'll be taste-testing them this weekend, so my brain won't be in great shape over the weekend. I can help on Monday, but I have to be here on Tuesday, then I can rejoin your team full time on Wednesday."

"Got it. This is a complicated case and it's not going to be solved by the weekend. What's your impression of Detective Greenwood?"

"It's actually positive. She gave me the usual stink eye at the start, but quickly found I was useful. She's not in the way at all for me, and kudos to her for bring your agency in on the case."

"Got it," and they ended the call.

Just as Jill ended her call with the special agent, Nathan came downstairs for his first cup of coffee. She silently handed it to him and went back to typing on her computer. She spent some time looking at the two locations she had visited the previous day as well as the two communities located outside of San Jose. If she had to drive into the area later that day, she wouldn't have time for computer work then.

She was lost in diving down rabbit holes when Nathan asked, "Did you have breakfast?"

Normally her answer was yes, but she had forgotten in her pursuit of emails and then her conversation with Leticia Ortiz. Nathan always asked when he was about to make breakfast for himself and upwards of 80 percent of the time the answer was "yes," but today was a rare occasion.

"I haven't. Thanks for asking. When I woke up I dived into emails and then I just had a call with Special Agent Leticia Ortiz."

He stopped for a minute thinking about what she'd told him about the case, and said, "That was rather soon, wasn't it? It didn't seem like you had much evidence, or suspects, and no one has tried to kill you."

"Yes to all three of those usual boxes that I tick before she gets involved. It's just a strange case as there's a corporation somehow involved and it's a highly unusual murder weapon, and it's likely to extend beyond the jurisdiction of San Jose shortly."

"Do you have to cancel our weekend to Paso Robles?" he asked as he was cracking eggs to make omelets.

"No. I told Leticia about that and the fact that my brain would likely not be in gear after all the wine tasting I needed to do. She has me today, tomorrow morning, and Monday, and then from Wednesday on next week." She loved that he didn't seem cranky that he might have to cancel plans he just made. She walked around their island to kiss him in thanks for being so understanding.

"Okay. I'll spend a little more time researching wineries to make sure I have the right line-up of your varietals."

"Are you visiting clients?"

"Nope. I'm just going to enjoy helping you taste-test. It will be your weekend to work."

"Do you already design for any of these vineyards?"

"No, these will be smaller vineyards for the most part. Much like your operation. They only have a tasting room open on the weekends. I think they're pursuing the same strategy as you by picking lesser-known varietals to compete against the big boys' and girls' operations."

"Does any operation have the exact same five that I picked?"

"No, you'll still be unique," Nathan said as he plated omelets, and she added toast to their plates.

"What are you up to today?" Jill asked.

"I've got client meetings starting in two hours and some zoom meetings. Are you heading over to San Jose?"

"Probably. Leticia was trying to round up people for a

meeting and said to stay available. I'll let you know if I'm not going to make it back for dinner, but I'm guessing that it will work out that way."

"Okay."

They finished their meal and cleaned the dishes, and Nathan was soon out the door. Jill decided to send a summary email to her teammates and then go for a run as the day would likely consist of a lot of sitting. Ten minutes later, she and Trixie were jogging slowly through the countryside. As she passed her empty acreage, she thought again about planting her varietals. Then her brain moved on to the case at hand.

She decided it was time to bring in the big guns. It was likely a challenge that her good friend Henrik Klein would enjoy. Henrik was based in Germany. He was a security and IT wizard. Several years ago, she solved the case of the death of his wife. She had had a nut allergy, and Jill had been sitting next to her in a restaurant in Antwerp and had resuscitated her and helped her make it alive to the hospital only to be murdered inside the hospital. Henrik had initially kidnapped Jill and her crew thinking they were somehow involved. Jill convinced him otherwise, and they had gone on to solve his wife's murder. Recently, Henrik and Marie were pursuing a relationship though he was in Germany, and she was in Wisconsin. They had even taken him to a Packers game. They vacationed with him in Canada and found a way to get together at least annually. Jill sat down to write an email to him. She had his phone number, but he frequently traveled the world so it might be the middle of the night wherever he was at the moment.

She asked him if he could use the image of the arsenic-filled water valve and an image of a mobile home in the location of the three states to determine when they showed up on satellite images. He was very good at searching for people and objects. He'd given Jill a copy of his personal identity software to use for her cases. He'd once commented that he should hire Jill as many law enforcements units after seeing it demonstrated by her on an actual case later sought to buy the software from him. She was curious to see what his answer would be on the water valve.

Her cell phone rang a moment later, and her caller ID let her know it was him. After she had explained her latest case and why she wanted such an obscure image searched, he understood her way of thinking.

"I love the challenges you throw at me. I get the most obscure requests from you," Henrik said in his German-accented English.

"I'm just trying to keep you on your toes. Where are you at the moment?" Jill asked, looking at her clock. It was mid-morning in California.

"I'm in Sweden."

"So, you're heading out to dinner?"

"Yes. Your query will stimulate our conversation. I'm meeting with the Swedish Police Authority, and while they have far less crime here, they'll still be interested as to whether my software can solve your question. I'll let you know if they say anything that might help your case. Meanwhile, I'll ask my staff if they can run your query. I might have an answer by the time I return from dinner."

"That's awesome, Henrik! We'll talk later. I don't want to delay your dinner. Who knows if the Swedes have an answer to this weird case."

"Jill, all your cases are weird. I'll talk to you later."

Jill smiled at Henrik's last comment. She had to admit that many of her cases were weird. She leaned back to think about it. She had poisonings, deliberate infections, head injuries, gunshot wounds, an ice arrow . . . her New Zealand murderer was creative with many methods, and a couple of more creative killers. Henrik was right, she concluded.

If the special agent arranged a meeting later today, the detective would likely have a result as to whether Mary Niles' neighbor had arsenic in his remains. The autopsy wouldn't be complete, but the first thing the Santa Clara Medical Examiner should do is a simple test for arsenic. It was time to search for the social media groups belonging to mobile home residents under threat of sale to HBX Builders. She wondered if there were more potential victims out there.

She found several groups and then used the search function to look for discussions about the sale of their community. It was incredibly tedious and sad work. People grieved the loss of their community. There was anger, denial, and every other emotion in the emails. Neighbors consoled each other and neighbors went into tirades against each other. It was painful sorting through the conversations for something useful. She had to read a lot of explosive words to understand who was slightly angry and who was destructively angry.

She felt her phone vibrate in her pocket and pulled it out to see who it was. It was a message from Leticia for a meeting time and place later that afternoon. She had about two more hours of research before she would have to leave. She was putting her phone away when she saw a new message from Henrik.

Still at dinner so can't talk but open your email—there is some video from my staff.

Jill opened her email box to find a message from an unknown sender. She clicked on that and found a short note and attachment with the logo of Henrik's company. This shouldn't be spam. She opened the attachment. There were tens of thousands of images from Nevada and Arizona. Entire mobile home parks had a valve on each incoming water main. Since she hadn't heard of an entire park dying, these must be legitimate users of a carbon filter. Maybe this was where the killer thought of his murder weapon. These were the original filters before someone removed the carbon and replaced them with arsenic. A quick search indicated the water was hard and mineral-filled in both of those states, thus the filters. Was their killer from one of those two states? Were any members of the leadership team at HBX from one of those two states? What could she do to get better data?

She'd been sitting for a while, so she got up and took a quick lap around her house and barns to stretch her legs and think about the problem. She settled back at her computer and asked the sender of the email to add one more variable: *send her pictures from parks that had three filters in them.* Perhaps that would aid her in telling which parks had carbon filters and which parks had the arsenic-modified filters. She sent the mail and decided it was time to head out for the meeting in San Jose. About a quarter of the way there, she received a call from Henrik.

"How was dinner?" Jill asked.

"Better for my business than yours."

"Sweden has committed to buying your software?"

"Yes. Sadly, they didn't have any ideas for your current case. However, it served to demonstrate how useful my software could be. The fact that I could produce tens of thousands of images had them cheering. When they heard about your modification, they tossed other ideas out but had nothing concrete to add. Perhaps you could call me with a case every time I have an important sales meeting, so I can demonstrate its advantages to my potential buyer. You won't take a marketing position within my company, but you could still help me demonstrate its value with obscure questions," Henrik said with humor in his voice.

"Every once in a while, I get a simple case with an obvious solution. That won't fit into your sales approach."

"No you don't. Every last one of your cases is strange. When I recounted some of your prior cases to the Swedish Police Authority, they didn't believe some of your outrageous stories until I produced newspaper articles verifying my story. In the end, they were happy *you live in America and don't bring your craziness to their country*. That's an exact quote."

Jill chuckled and said, "Did you remind them that some of those cases were in their nearby neighbors of the United Kingdom, Italy, and the Netherlands?"

"I did, and they said jokingly that they would put your name on a list that would deny your entry to their country."

"Some day when I visit Sweden, I might be calling you to get me out of being deported."

They joked a little while longer and then Henrik informed her that her revised run would be in her mailbox by the time she reached her destination.

CHAPTER 14

$\mathcal{J}$ill pulled into the lot where her meeting was supposed to take place. It was not police headquarters where she had met Detective Greenwood. Instead, it was about fifteen miles away in South San Jose and it was a training building, according to the signage on the outside. She was just grateful that there was plenty of parking nearby and if she got out of the meeting in time, she could jump into the big box store across the parking lot and pick up some supplies.

After entering the lobby, she was directed to a conference room on the second floor. She walked into the room and found Leticia and her staff already there. She was exchanging a hug with the Special Agent as Detectives Greenwood and Crawford walked in. She saw the detective's eyes raised at the hug.

"Do you two know each other?"

Leticia answered, "Yes, we've worked several cases together. Somehow, I'm not surprised that Dr. Quint is in the middle of this one. The strangest cases come from her. She's also worked with our offices in Denver and DC and I've served as her reference with the Italian and Australian police forces."

"Interesting," Greenwood said, unable to think of any other comment. She'd rarely worked with civilians on cases and most of the time it was a disaster. It was good to know that this case wouldn't likely go sideways because of the actions of this civilian.

"Who else are we waiting on?" Jill asked, not knowing who was invited.

"Our ME and my LT."

Jill nodded. Her past experience with wide-ranging cases had department supervisors getting involved once an outside agency like the FBI was involved.

The final two attendees arrived, and introductions were performed. They started with the Santa Clara County Medical Examiner, as he had more autopsies awaiting his return to his building to complete. Besides, he had a small role in this case and there was no need for him to stay for the briefing.

"Let's start with Dr. Hughes. Doctor, what have you found in your limited time with our victims' remains? We'll get his report out of the way so he can leave and get back to his large caseload at the morgue," Greenwood said.

"I can confirm the presence of arsenic. One of my aides is looking into his employment record to make sure he didn't work in an arsenic-laden industry like mining. However, I suspect he'll become your second victim."

The group asked a few more questions, then he left to return to the morgue.

Jill had been searching her email for the update from Henrik's company. She opened the spreadsheet and saw that the tens of thousands of photos had been reduced to fewer than twenty. Jill doubted there were twenty victims in this case, as surely it would have been discovered before now.

Jill raised her hand that she had new knowledge. She explained who Henrik was and that she had asked his software engineers to search for the valve and then gave the results of that first search. A few people were looking either impressed or skeptical that Jill had thought to look at this piece of data. She then connected her laptop to the room's projector and brought up the photos. Each photo contained the geocoordinates of its location so they would be able to look up the mobile home community. Crawford was taking notes of locations, so Jill assumed the detective would end up with the assignment of running down these communities.

"So, our killer may have had experience with these filters in the past. It sounds like they are in wide use," Greenwood said.

"Yes. I didn't ask for a run of all locations with these water valves, but I can't imagine that the pressure from the water main at a mobile home park is much different from that going to a single-family home. I'll ask for that run just to clear up whether our killer likely gained knowledge of those carbon filter valves because he or she lived in a mobile home park," Jill said while composing an email to Henrik to ask for that data.

"Detective, did you test the valve you found in the trash dumpster for arsenic?" the lieutenant asked.

"Yes sir. It came back positive for arsenic. So, we have a hit on our murder weapon, but we don't know which house had the valve if indeed any did. Perhaps our perp dumped it at the site."

"Did you find any fingerprints on any of the valves?" Jill asked.

"We did. They are too numerous to prove much of anything. Besides, you said you solve all your cases in under a month and we wouldn't get back results for potentially longer than that period of time."

A little snark by Detective Greenwood. Oh well, she had expected it at some point in the case.

"How about the arsenic? Was it exactly the same in every filter?" Jill asked, ignoring the detective's comment.

"That's a good question. I'm not sure what the answer tells us, though."

"It may be related to the length of time in any set of pipes, or whether our killer was experimenting and watching the impact on mobile home residents," Jill said.

"That's a chilling thought," Crawford said.

"Special Agent Ortiz, will your BAU [behavioral analysis unit] be providing an assessment of these murders and any others we discover going forward related to arsenic-contaminated water valves?" the lieutenant asked. "I, at least, do not have a picture of the murder suspect in my mind,"

"That's an interesting question. Does anyone in this room have a vision of the murder suspect?" Ortiz asked.

Throughout the room, people shook their heads, including Jill. Even though woman were more prone to poison, she somehow thought this was a male suspect if for no other reason than it took hand strength to change that plumbing pipe. She thought about tossing out her comment but decided that it didn't add to the case, and she stayed silent.

"Dr. Quint, what is going to be your approach with the photos of water valves?" Ortiz asked.

"I'll locate each mobile home park first. If any are still standing, I'll focus on them. Someone is likely being poisoned in that community. We need to save their life first, then analyze the community. Maybe if it is still occupied, there may be camera footage or other evidence of who inserted the valve. Also, some of these locations may be mobile home parks that aren't for sale or are being taken over by a different contractor than HBX Builders."

"That's a good plan," Ortiz said. "So we don't duplicate anyone's work, I'll speak for my staff when I say we'll search our extensive archives to look for another crime like this one and we'll have the BAU give us a reading.

Jill and the special agent turned to look at the SJPD staff.

The lieutenant spoke for the group and said, "We'll need to determine if any of these locations are in our jurisdiction. If they're not, then we'll brief the police force in charge of that area."

The meeting wrapped up as soon as the division of work was assigned. Jill looked at her watch and decided the freeways were heating up. If she left now, she would still be caught in traffic, but it would be a lot less miserable than about ninety minutes from now. She left the parking lot and found the nearest freeway ramp to get her in an easterly direction just before she left. She would be home early enough for them to share their dinner.

While she was driving, she was thinking about the case and looking occasionally at her rear-view mirror for any emergency vehicles that she would need to pull over for, but the drive remained clear. She was startled when she heard a bang nearby. In the lane next to her, one car had hit the one in front of it with surprising force. She debated whether she should stop and administer first aid. In that short time of her considering her options, traffic had easily moved on by almost half a mile and growing. If she pulled over and carried her medical bag back to the victims, she might risk an accident herself. As much as she wanted to help, there were closer people in the long line of traffic behind her. She dialed 911 just to make sure the accident was called into the emergency dispatch. Eventually, she made it out of Silicon Valley and over the Diablo Mountains to the central valley. She knew that many people who were driving near her made this commute every day. She couldn't imagine a ninety-minute to two-hour commute twice a day. It was housing prices that drove people so far out. She made a mental note to look up the accident when she got home. Mostly she wanted to know if she would have made a difference if she had stopped.

Nathan beat her home and was cooking dinner. She smelled

the barbeque and made a bet in her head that it was going to be steak, vegetables, and potatoes, all cooked to perfection in the barbeque. After she greeted the dog, she moved on to kiss Nathan. Trixie acted like a roadblock and demanded she be acknowledged first. To be fair, the dog was in her life first, so she understood the dog's behavior, but she'd rather kiss Nathan.

After their kiss, she looked over at the kitchen island and smiled when her menu guess was correct.

"Why are you smiling? Are you craving steak tonight?" Nathan asked.

"No. I smelled the barbeque outside and made a bet with myself about what your menu would be tonight, and I guessed right."

"That's a good guess, though I admit that I almost bought chicken for tonight. How did your meeting go?"

"Special Agent Leticia and I were exchanging a hug when the detective walked in, so I grew creds from the fact I know the local FBI well enough to hug its officers."

Nathan smiled at her comment and asked, "Are we still on for Paso Robles this weekend?"

"Yep. I need to do more computer work, but there's nothing I need to move this case along that I can't do remotely. What time do you want to leave tomorrow?"

"We can't check into the hotel until three. There's one winery on the way that will have two of your wines, so we can stop there. How about a noon departure?"

"Sounds like a plan. I'll pack my bag, then I'm going to research some photos that Henrik's company sourced for me. I asked him if he could do a computer search looking for a mobile home that might have the arsenic-laden water valve in California, Arizona, and Nevada. It came back with tens of thousands of photos as the filter is used frequently in Nevada and Arizona. They have water systems that are hard and contain lots of minerals. Then I revised it to look for mobile home parks that had no more than three valves per park and he came back with about twenty locations. I'm worried that someone right now is actively being poisoned with arsenic."

"From what you've told me about the case, I guess I'd be worried too. At least whoever is your murderer isn't likely to attack you or this property. That will be a pleasant change."

"Yes, with this case we're all safe."

They had a delicious dinner, accompanied by wine made with one of the varietals she was considering. Nathan, her ever-thoughtful husband, visited a local wine seller and bought five different vineyard's vintages of one of the varietals she was considering. So they had a nice blind taste testing with their dinner. Nathan looked up the rating for the wines, and Jill correctly lined up the wines in order of rating. To her that said that she could be the taste master for this varietal and make a wine that would be highly rated. She went upstairs to their bedroom to pack her suitcase for the weekend, and then came back downstairs to her computer to look at the geolocations of the photos. She guessed that by now the police had already gone through the list and knew if someone was at risk of poisoning.

She leaned back and thought about it and decided to call Detective Crawford to see if she found anything on the locations. If she hadn't had time to look them all up yet, then Jill might focus on the photos she hadn't gotten to yet. Finding the location of the photo on a map was easy. The question was whether the mobile home park was still there and, if not, who had bought the land.

She waited about twenty minutes and had no reply from the detective. So, did Detective Crawford turn her email off at a certain hour, or was she not paying attention to it because she was searching for the photo locations? Regardless, Jill started from the bottom of the list and started searching. She was serious about looking for someone who was a rabble rouser in their community but was being slowly poisoned. Maybe they could save a life. Her second location from the bottom of the list seemed like it might be in the process of a takeover. She did some more checking and then used a search to find photos beyond the satellite to check on the community. She thought the park might still be there, which meant that someone might be in active danger. She picked up her phone to call Detective Greenwood.

The call was answered and Jill said, "Detective, I think you need to check on a community right away."

"I'm on my way to a community now. What's the address of the one you found?"

Jill gave the address, and she was relieved to hear it was the same location the detective was heading to.

CHAPTER 15

Jill waited to hear from the detective but fell asleep before she informed her of what was happening. She awoke the next morning to a text.

Found water valve. Victims at hospital getting checked out.
Your computer search saved a life or two tonight.

Wow! Jill thought there must be two people living in the mobile home and that was a first. So far, their victims had lived in single-occupancy homes. The text was sent at one in the morning, so Jill thought it was likely a bad time to call the detective. Her clock read six, so she would wait to call until nine. She opened her email app and saw lots of correspondence related to the case. Greenwood, Crawford, Ortiz, Henrik, and Marie all had sent something for her to read.

Detective Crawford returned the answer to her question. She started from the top with an eye toward identifying who might be in her jurisdiction first. She'd found the problematic location a little before Jill and Crawford had dispatched the detective and water company to the location. She then returned to the list and began notifying other law enforcements agencies of the problem. The FBI was backing up Crawford as when she initially made calls, some agencies asked for her badge number and then called and verified that she was a detective, thinking her call was a hoax. As at least one of the locations was out of state, the FBI had a firm role in bridging the states. Of the list of twenty, four of the parks were still occupied. Local law enforcement was approaching each of the parks.

Jill sent an email to Henrik as he had asked for an update. He and his staff should know that his software had saved lives in the United States. She also thought he should route the real-life example of how powerful his software was to the law enforcement folks from Sweden since they knew of the conversation. Actually, the more she thought about it, the more she believed he should make a case study of her experience for all future sales. She knew Henrik well enough to know he wouldn't be offended as the CEO with her suggesting a sales strategy.

Greenwood passed on the preliminary medical examiner's report. A final report would be released in a few weeks once some testing results were reported. It noted skin pigment changes and GI tract changes consistent with arsenic poisoning. The detective also mentioned that she notified the family, and they would be coming in later that day for an interview. There was nothing for Jill to do with that knowledge.

So far, she really appreciated the detectives keeping her in the loop. It seemed in most cases she had to beg for information and often hit a wall. Maybe if she had any future cases with this police force, she would not have to reestablish her credentials and benefit to their case before she gained cooperation.

Moving on to the email from Leticia Ortiz, she had suggested daily video calls to keep the team up to date starting today at one in the afternoon, and she included a link for the call. Jill replied that she would be on the road at that time and would participate as cellular coverage allowed. Ortiz also shared a preliminary assessment from the Behavior Analysis Unit. It was an attachment, so Jill would open that after reading the rest of the email. The special agent briefed her colleagues in the regions beyond the San Francisco region where some of the active mobile home parks were located. She noted that one of the parks was within her region and her staff were on scene working with the locals. The home where the valve was found contained two occupants who were at the hospital being evaluated. They both had some gastrointestinal signs of arsenic poisoning.

Jill moved on to the attachment. The initial assessment confirmed her thoughts—their suspect was of an unknown gender. While poison was the choice of females, as this appeared to be a serial killer as they now had evidence of more than three victims, they felt their suspect was more likely male and was working alone. They weren't clear if this job was hired out or if the suspect was doing their own work. Regardless, the suspect had a science background to have arrived at this use of arsenic. While arsenic has been used for many murders over the centuries, they had no records of someone inserting the element into a water filter. The report also said it was rare in recent times for a corporation to hire out the work. There were examples of corporate malfeasance related to organized crime, but not in recent decades. They would have more details in a later report. Jill leaned back in her chair after reading the assessment and concluded the only piece of new information was the tie of the behavior to earlier times and organized crime.

Finally, she opened Marie's email. She'd found more social media groups for Jill to read about in the most recent locations from the twenty or so photos. Marie, being a social media maven, had used a search function and copied some key conversations regarding a resident not feeling well.

Jill was helping herself to a second cup of coffee and leaning against the counter near her coffee pot thinking about all the new information, which didn't help her much to form a picture of the suspect in her mind, other than a stereotype of a scientist with wild hair and bubbling test tubes. She looked up as Nathan walked into the kitchen.

He leaned in to kiss her, then took her coffee mug for that first sip of life-altering caffeine. He passed the cup back to her and said, "Thanks and good morning." That was being conversational in the early morning for Nathan.

"You're more awake than usual for this time of day. What's up?"

"I slept well, and we have a great day ahead of us. That is assuming we can still get away?" Nathan asked with a question. He knew that when she was in the middle of the case her plans could change on the fly.

"We're getting away. I'll take a video call from the car at one and I warned them I would be traveling in my car at that time and would be subject to the whims of cellular service."

"Awesome. We have a four o'clock tasting reservation with a winery near Paso Robles and I know you like a clear head for your law enforcement conversations. Any new news on the case?"

"Actually, some really cool news. Police intervened late last night at four mobile home parks which had arsenic-laden water valves. I let Henrik know that his software saved lives."

"Can hospitals reverse the damage from arsenic if it hasn't killed someone yet?" Nathan asked.

Wow, Jill thought, his brain was really engaged this morning for him to remember the details of the case.

"Some damage, yes. It depends on how close to death the body is—how much cellular damage they have that can't be repaired."

"So getting those victims to medical care should save their lives."

"Yes."

"You thought of searching satellite photos, so you should take at least half the credit for saving lives. Yes, it was Henrik's powerful software that processed it, but you asked the right questions of the computer. Did that break the ice for you with law enforcement?"

Nathan knew that her struggle in almost any case was getting a "new to her" law enforcement unit to trust her expertise. That lack of trust led to frustration and often slowed a homicide case to be solved.

"It did break the ice as you say. Two detectives volunteered new information to me in an email overnight."

"That's a great way to start your day. I'm going to head to work for a client meeting. I'll pass our housesitting key to Peter. I should be back home no later than noon. I'll grab us some sandwiches to eat along the way, so we have a food base before drinking wine. Depending on where we are at the time of your call, we could pull over to a rest stop and picnic while you converse as long as they have cellular."

"Awesome. That sounds like a great plan. I'll make up the bedroom for the house sitter and pack a cooler for us. This was a great idea. Thank you for thinking about it."

Nathan left and Jill returned to thinking about how she could find their suspect. Since he committed the crime weeks to months before his victim died, how did they find the man? Maybe one of the recent mobile home communities still had security cameras. She shot an email to Detective Greenwood and Special Agent Ortiz with a suggestion that they focus on video coverage. Also, perhaps if she could interview the newest victims, she might be able to lock down when the valve was inserted, assuming it contained arsenic and that it was legitimately placed to filter water. She needed to back up and verify that the valve did contain their agent and noted that question to the FBI as they were coordinating the other locations.

Needing some thinking time, she moved on to getting the house ready for their sitter. Fortunately, he had house sat many times for them, so she didn't need to leave elaborate instructions. The animals were in good hands. She put their suitcases in the car and pulled out the cooler. She included a few samples of her latest vintage in case she had time to sell to any wine stores along the way. She also packed an empty wine bottle box with room for them to purchase twelve bottles. Then, since Trixie was looking so sad at the usual signs of the dog's human owners leaving, Jill took her out into the vineyard so she could study where she would plant which varietals while the dog chased squirrels. There was nothing like a good squirrel chase to improve Trixie's mood.

Meanwhile, she thought about how she was going to find the murderer. Could it be a hired assassin—an old-fashioned murder-for-hire operation with someone high up in the investor company pulling the strings? It was an intriguing comment by the FBI. What was the connection to the company? Was someone trying to set up the company to look like the murderer? If someone else was mad at the company, weren't there easier ways to make the company look bad? Also, who would have access to which mobile home parks the company was trying to acquire? That was insider knowledge. Until the sale went through and that was reflected in public records, who else but a company employee would have access to which communities were under consideration? Furthermore, who would know which of the residents would become leaders of the resistance to the sale of the community?

She returned inside and found an email from Greenwood. The location of the mobile home community that she visited the previous night had a water valve that tested positive for arsenic. They hadn't heard back from the other new locations, and they were not sure they would as the FBI had taken over communicating with those folks.

She went back to the pictures that her search had provided. Were any of these communities not under consideration of HBX Builders? Did any of these communities have a lack of conversations about their park being sold? Were all of these communities set up as land rental communities? She sent emails to Marie and Jo with the latest update and a request that they both search for the answer to her questions. Meanwhile she began a search in a couple of real estate websites to see if prior listings in these parks described the rental fee.

She worked her way through the list and was halfway finished when Nathan arrived home. They departed shortly while a very sad-looking Trixie and an indifferent Arthur watched. Nathan's assistant would arrive in a few hours and then they would be happy. On their way to Paso Robles, there would be a stretch of highway that was straight, and she thought she could finish her real estate search then, assuming she had cellular service. First, they had a few twists and turns to reach that straight stretch of road, and Jill would quickly become carsick if she tried to do any work on her phone. So she set aside the work and chatted about planning a trip to Wisconsin to see her friends in the future. Nathan was tied to California now that he was a professor at the university, so unless he was on an academic break, they were unable to travel together except for long weekends.

Once they hit the straight section of the interstate, she finished her search before their scheduled appointment time. She verified that about half of the communities where the photos were taken were land rental arrangements. She made a note to call a real estate agent and ask how sales of the whole community occurred. Was there something in the community's bylaws that allowed for a vote of perhaps two-thirds or three-quarters of the community members agreeing to a sale? Something to think about.

Jill checked her time and her cellular coverage. It was good at the moment, but as she looked at the mountains to her right, she knew that she would have no reception inside them. There was a rest stop about three miles away and her phone call was supposed to take place in about fifteen minutes. That would give them time to stop and find a picnic table. Her worry was with the noise of an interstate, would she be able to hear? She had brought earbuds with her, so hopefully that would work. It was sunny and about sixty degrees, so good weather to eat outdoors.

Nathan grabbed the picnic basket along with two bottles of water. Jill had her laptop having already tested the Wi-Fi at the rest area. They were all set for a delicious lunch and a video call. Jill decided to spend a little more time with her video call settings, so she soon had a background that looked like someone's home library rather than the bleak sandy-looking background of the California rest stop. Some rest stops were designed with separate parking areas for large semi-tractors and passenger vehicles. So, while she might find the picnic table farthest from the interstate, if the large trailers with their diesel engines and air brakes were nearby, that noise would be worse. She thought about heading out to the sand as Nathan had a picnic blanket, but she might then be beyond the range of the Wi-Fi. She and Nathan spoke as they set up their lunch and she could hear his words, so that was best she could do given the ambient noise at this location.

She had a few bites of a delicious turkey, Swiss cheese, and avocado sandwich on a wonderful bread. Then she used the link to connect to the call. After everyone joined, Leticia set a quick agenda—an update from anyone with new information including what happened in the other jurisdictions where potential victims were located. She also announced that the Behavior Analysis Unit had not completed their assessment of the murderer given the unusual circumstances.

Leticia ran an efficient meeting, and they were finished in less than forty-five minutes. Jill decided to turn off her video as it improved her reception for the call and allowed her to finish her lunch without everyone on the call watching her chew.

In total, Jill's search for photos had saved the lives of five people. After interviewing residents of the mobile home parks, law enforcement developed a list of an additional six people who had been spokespersons against the sale of the property and who neighbors felt had died before their time. They were now researching whether the remains were available for exhumation.

"Wait a minute," Jill interrupted. "These people that a mobile home community thought had died before their time should have had a valve in line to their trailer. This is a new factor of behavior if the killer is returning and removing the valve."

There was silence on the call while everyone thought of the implication of the killer returning to remove the arsenic-ladened water valve.

"Did they change their process? Special Agent Ortiz, where were these communities in the process of being sold? At the beginning or at the end? I ask because in the community here in San Jose, the battle over that sale had been going on for four to five years. Our victim, Mary Niles, died last week and the valve was still in place. So the killer didn't come back to remove it or the other valve for the other resident who was thought to die before his time. Does that mean there are two killers who have a slightly different process?" Greenwood asked of the group.

"Those are good questions, Detective. I'll have my staff put together a timeline of when we think that a sale of the mobile home community came to the residents' attention, what the dates of death were, and what kind of arrangement concerning the land existed—whether it was owned by the homeowner or if the residents paid rent for the land. I'll add that to the information the BAU is examining to develop a probable description of our perp."

The call ended shortly after that comment, and Jill and Nathan cleaned up their picnic and hit the road.

CHAPTER 16

They arrived at the vineyard which was located in the Temblor Range between the San Joaquin Valley and the Central Coast leading into Paso Robles. The vineyard was available for taste testing by appointment only. Jill read about the winery and knew their model was similar to hers. They sold two of the varietals that were on Jill's list to expand her vineyard. She had a taste of their Syrah and their Marsala. She questioned the vineyard owner about growing the varietals as every grape had its quirks. She walked away with a bottle of each, and they were on their way to their hotel for check in.

They were on the outskirts of the town when Jill noticed a mobile home park. She said to Nathan, "Make a left turn into that community, please," pointing to the mobile homes. He did as she asked and asked, "Where to?"

"I would like to see if there are any arsenic valves on any of the homes and ask the residents if they're aware of anyone they think passed before their time."

"I thought you had Henrik do a run for you and this location wasn't on your list?"

"I did, but it occurs to me that I did the wrong thing. I asked for any mobile home park that had three valves. I should have asked for three or less, meaning this park might have one or two mobile homes with valves, but they didn't show up on my list because I asked for three valves. The computer only spits out the data you ask it to. Since we're driving past and someone might be in danger, let me take a quick look inside."

Nathan drove very slowly so she could look at the plumbing for each mobile home. They had a few people staring back at them, so Jill rolled down her window and said to the next concerned community member, "I've been thinking of moving to a mobile home community. I'm looking at the various configurations here."

Her response was created by suspicion, but someone pointed her to a home at the end of the street. "That one's for sale. The owner died last month."

Alarms bells rang loudly in her head as she thanked the resident for information. Nathan continued slowly down the street.

"People die in mobile home parks all the time. Granted it is usually from tornadoes or fires, but that's not the case for this home as I can see it's intact," Jill said as she examined each water connection going into the homes. She was lucky that this wasn't a climate that required the pipes to be covered to prevent freezing as that would have prevented her from seeing the connections.

"It's interesting that that woman said the home was for sale. Why would it be for sale if the entire community was about to be sold?" Nathan asked.

"Maybe it's just a coincidence that there's a unit for sale. I imagine most parks have at least one unit for sale most of the time, as it takes the right buyer to want to spend money on such a home."

The way this community was constructed, the front of the homes faced each other so she needed to drive both directions on each street in this development so she could examine the pipes. They reached the end of the street and saw the for-sale sign in front of the home.

"Let's pause a moment here," Jill said. She got out of the car to look at the mobile home and in particular the valve she could see in the water line. She took a picture of it, added the address, and sent it to Special Agent Ortiz and Detective Greenwood. The police would need to come and examine this community. She knew if she made the call to the local police, she would be labeled as a lunatic. Right now she wanted to finish examining the community's homes and then she would retreat with Nathan to their hotel. She also knew that she needed a revised search by Henrik's people to look for communities with one or two valves. She pulled up her email stating the parameters of the search and sure enough her wording was incomplete.

She got back into their car to continue looking at the homes on the opposite side of the street. She had Nathan pause again when her phone rang, and the caller ID said it was Leticia Ortiz.

"Hello, Special Agent."

"It's Leticia. You're scaring me. You decide to randomly tour a mobile home community you pass on the way to your hotel, and you find another valve. I used to say your mere presence attracted the killer in any case. With this case you seem to be a few steps behind them. Why wasn't this location on our original search? I looked, and the address wasn't there."

"I gave the wrong parameters to the analyst doing the search. I was so overwhelmed by the thousands of valves legitimately in line in mobile home parks that I picked the random number of three valves to include in my search. I should have said three or less. I'll probably run into problems with that search as there may be many mobile home communities wherein one resident had tried to improve their water quality by correctly using this valve. I'll be sending an email to the analyst to rerun the search after I finish driving through this community."

"Got it. I've got to contact my colleague in Los Angeles as

this is his territory. I know you're on vacation, but I'm still going to give him your contact information."

"That's fine. I'm going through the community as we speak as I want to see if there are any other valves. Then I'll request a revised search requested from my data person to see how big the problem is. Of course, I don't know if this is a bad valve, but it is suspicious, and the owner is dead. I didn't call the police here locally as I'm sure the call would be viewed as a crank call."

"Sadly, I think you're right. As the owner is dead, and you haven't found another valve as yet, there's no healthcare emergency yet. I hope it stays that way. How many of the mobile home communities had just one valve in them? Do you remember from your list?"

"No, that's the whole problem with my list as I asked for communities with three valves. I should have recognized the problem immediately, as the community of our first victim—Mary Niles—had two valves in it."

"Okay, I'll keep you posted."

They ended the call, and Nathan continued his slow drive through the community. There was a newer part of the community where the water valves were in the back of the homes rather than in the front. That made sense from an aesthetic perspective, but it meant that Jill would have to get out of her car and individually walk into the private space of each homeowner. She passed on that activity knowing that law enforcement would arrive later that day. She sent a follow-up email to Leticia explaining her process. Then she took care of the new run she needed from Henrik's analyst.

Nathan and Jill continued to the next vineyard where they also had an appointment. Their hotel check-in was delayed by Jill's side trip into the mobile home community.

"You must be grateful that we didn't pass any additional mobile home parks to further delay our vacation."

"I've learned to literally roll with the punches when you're on a case. We have no schedule this weekend after this upcoming appointment, as the remainder of the wineries are open scheduled hours for tasting. So we're all good here. Besides, who knows what law enforcement will find? Our little detour may have saved someone's life."

"Sweetie, that is one of the many reasons I love you. You're not angry that yet another case has disrupted a vacation."

"Actually, except for that tour through the mobile home park, our vacation hasn't been disrupted," Nathan said, following his GPS to turn into the next vineyard.

Again, it was a private tour as this was another small winery. It featured Sangiovese and Syrah wines. Jill repeated her questions for this owner, sampled their wine, and walked away with a bottle of each varietal.

Their next stop was their hotel. They brought their wine inside with the luggage as it wouldn't be good for it to sit inside a sun heated vehicle even in the fall. Their plan was to visit a larger winery and sample their varietals, then head for dinner, and finish the evening up with live music at another winery.

Normal people might be tipsy with the amount they'd consumed that day, but Jill was a seasoned wine taster. When she was at home tasting her varietals, she walked with a spittoon as she tasted, but didn't swallow the wine. When at other wineries, spitting was frowned upon, so she managed to form an opinion about a wine with a minimal amount and dumped the remainder of the poured wine into whatever receptacle the winery had nearby.

After unloading their belongings, they headed back to the car to continue to the next winery. Henrik's analyst sent her another run, and it was concerning. It came back with a list of over two hundred locations. Yeah, she thought they had a serial killer on their hands, but this seemed an extreme way he or she might have set up that many people to die. Some of the historically worst serial killers reached three to four hundred people and she hoped that was not what they had on their hands. She was scrolling through the list just to get a sense of the data. The FBI would have its hands full running down the many potential locations of arsenic filters. She forwarded the list to everyone who had been on that afternoon's call so they could all go to work looking for potential victims.

"What is your sigh for?" Nathan asked as he pulled into the winery's parking lot.

"The latest run from Henrik's company lists over two hundred locations in three states. I'm hopeful that some of these locations are carbon filters for water rather than arsenic-laden filters."

"Wow, if your pro-bono case explodes into the unveiling of a serial killer of that magnitude, that will splash your name all over the press and make every law enforcement agency take you seriously. Of course, it's terrible that so many people may have lost their lives to this killer as is the case with any serial killer."

"Yes. This is going to explode quickly. I think I'll send an email to Catherine Dobson to update her on the coming storm as well as to Marie, Jo, and Angela. Let me take a minute to compose my messages and then, with this tasting, I'll swallow more wine than usual. This computer run is bad news."

"Have you reached out to the manufacturer to see who made a two-to-three-hundred-unit purchase of those valves? Surely there's not a large list of people who buy that many?" Nathan said.

"That's a good question that I'll send to my law enforcement partners. When this case was one or two valves in different cities, it would have been impossible to trace. Now that we have the potential for hundreds, you have to think our killer made a bulk purchase. Let me add that question to my email list," Jill said.

Nathan parked the car and was viewing the emails on his

phone while Jill dictated a message to each group that she wanted to send emails to with questions or updates.

"Finished! Let's go inside," Jill said and exited the car. It was time to switch gears and think about the business side of things.

She grasped Nathan's hand and stood looking at the winery's tasting room, parking lot, and an area being set up for food trucks and an outdoor concert. It was probably similar to what they were planning to attend later that evening. She could smell the wine from the parking lot, and she liked what she smelled.

"I don't like their tasting room design—it looks rather bland and industrial, but I like the wine scent in the air. It also looks like many of these wineries have tastings by day and live music and food in the evening. I don't see my winery ever getting to that point. That's a big operation."

"Yes. I like the small tasting rooms we encountered in Sicily. The vineyards were operated by families with farm helpers, and the family ran the tasting room. That would be hard for you to do, but maybe you can work out an arrangement with another winery to swap hours with you helping them or they staff your tasting room. I don't see you creating a music venue and food truck party."

As they opened the door to walk inside, Jill agreed. "You're right about me not wanting to create a food and music destination. I want to remain small and intimate with just a few good wines. I don't think I want to add a bottling room. I think I'd rather continue to hire that service."

Nathan nodded as they stepped up to the bar to begin their tasting. She had a flight of five wines that included two varietals under consideration by her.

"Is this winery a customer of yours?" Jill asked, examining the labels on the wine bottles. She could usually recognize a Nathan wine label design, but he had his imitators.

"They were clients, but one of the family members was a

student in my program at the university and they took over designing for the winery about a year ago. So the newer labels aren't mine, but I think the family is lucky to have that skill among their members. She can also create marketing materials on the dime when they need it. I'm happy for them as that proves the success of the university program."

"And they're lucky to find that kind of creativity in a family member," Jill said, knowing that the drawing and creating marketing materials skill was a gene she was missing. If she were in charge of her labels, she would never sell a bottle of wine.

They finished their tastings and again purchased a few bottles. Now they were heading to a ranch for a farm-to-table dinner. Jill liked the freshness of that kind of food and the communal conversations you had with people seated around you. She took a look at her phone and observed that she had many messages awaiting a reply. She looked at the time and decided she would have to silence her phone and occasionally read the messages while they were at dinner. It would be rude to stare at the phone while an excellent meal was being prepared, but perhaps she could catch a peep every now and then. If she stayed in the car, they would be late, and if she tried to read the messages on the curvy road, she would have been too carsick to enjoy the meal. Besides, it was unlikely that anything she did for the case in the next ninety minutes would make a difference in the outcome of the case.

"You're doing a great job ignoring your phone. I'm impressed."

"This is our quickie vacation. I'm already making you work on my other job as a vineyard owner by focusing on particular varietals. It would be extremely rude to ignore you and become one with my cell phone. So I'm going to sneak the odd peek at what people are sending me, but overall I'm going to try and be present at our dinner."

Nathan smiled at her and rubbed her shoulder as they began walking toward the tent hosting their dinner. They found their seats across from each other. Nathan observed Jill peeking at her phone whenever the chef took a moment to talk about the meal, the food, the wine pairings, and the farm. When the chef was quiet, Jill left her phone in her pocket and engaged with Nathan and the people sitting around them.

CHAPTER 17

"That was a great choice for a meal. The chef was able to talk about the food without sounding snooty. What kind of music is our next venue hosting?"

"It's Bluegrass and Zydeco. I know those aren't your favorite types of music, but it's good to expand your horizons on occasion."

"You're right that I don't listen to that type of music, but hey, maybe I'll like it."

"I suspect you won't hear the first twenty minutes as you'll be immersed in your emails," Nathan said with a smile.

"You know me well. Thanks for putting up with my preference for murder investigations over almost anything."

"I know that once you take care of your business, you'll be all in to enjoy the music and the night. Should I get us a bottle of wine?"

"How about just a glass each? I'm starting to feel the effects of our wine tasting and the wine served with dinner. I'm afraid I might grab a guitar and try to play if I have much more alcohol in my system. As I don't have a musical bone in my body, you know what a disaster that would be."

Nathan laughed in agreement and left to fetch two glasses of wine. They had lawn chairs and expected to be at the location for about two hours. That was plenty of time to sip and for Jill to respond to her messages. He returned just before the music started, and she had made her way through about half of the messages. She decided to start with easy ones first. Catherine Dobson was pleased that her action to ask Jill to look at the case resulted in lives being saved in other mobile home communities. There was no need to reply to Catherine.

Next, she opened the special agent's email. After thanking her for the revised data, her team wondered if Jill had any suggestions on how to prioritize the locations as there were so many of them to follow up on. Jill's foot was swinging to the music as she thought about the answer to Leticia's question, then she had a suggestion.

> *Prioritize based on the date of the picture.*
> *Survey homes with the oldest dates as they*
> *have the longest potential exposure to arsenic.*

Leticia replied with her thanks and so Jill went on to the next inquiry, from Detective Greenwood. She said the criminalist assigned to the case said all of their valves were the same model number. They called the company, but they don't sell direct. The police were given a list of suppliers that were their distributors. They began calling those companies, but it took a while to weave through large distributors to find the person who knew which stores had large purchases. Of course, their killer could have paid cash and bought the valves in groups of ten. After all, it took time to modify and install each valve, so there wasn't a need for the killer to keep a huge inventory. The detective thought it was going to take days to get answers, and the answers wouldn't necessarily pinpoint the killer.

Jill asked for the model of the valve as her hotel was near a few of the big box home improvement stores. She was curious enough to buy one and study it. She thought it might lead her to a new clue about the killer.

Finally, she moved on to the responses from her friends. Of course, they offered to be on standby for any research Jill needed as they were all appalled at the breadth of this killing spree. All murderers were horrible, but there was something especially horrific about going after a bunch of senior citizens who were trying to protect their forever homes. Jo couldn't think of any financial research she could do as she had exhausted the search for HBX Builders, and Marie said something similar. Angela was sitting on the sidelines as her greatest skills were in photography and interviewing. They had few suspects and witnesses so far in this case.

Still, Jill thought about the company. She asked Jo and Marie to do searches of the respective people on the leadership team and board of directors for the company. Maybe that would reveal who the killer was in leadership. She wouldn't get answers from them tonight, but maybe the weekend would yield some new information.

She tuned into the music, hoping to refresh her brain by enjoying the sounds of the band. She looked over at Nathan and saw that he was relaxed and wiggling his knee to the music. She grasped his hand and smiled at him, pleased that her mate wasn't at all perturbed with her doing a murder investigation while they sat in slouchy chairs under the stars surrounded by a vineyard. It was too romantic a setting for her to be focused on murder.

He raised his eyebrows in question, and she whispered into his ear, "Here we are in the classic California romantic setting and you're enjoying the music while I'm investigating a serial killer and we're both content. Love you."

"It's all part of the package of being with you. Besides, I was thinking of adding a sketch of a band in the vineyard for one of my upcoming labels for a client. Specifically for you—how about if at the launch of your new varietals, we consider the five varietals to represent different instruments in a band and build a story around that?"

She gave him a huge grin and nodded in agreement. She thought his idea brilliant, and she liked that he could work on ideas while she worked on murder in the same setting.

She hugged his upper arm and then relaxed back to listen to the remainder of the set. The band took a break, so now they could talk freely.

"I love your idea about music. Of course, as the vintner I should have an interest in these musical instruments, but since I'm musically inept, you'll have to the carry the weight. However, I'll start thinking about a story. I can think of other vineyards that have linked their wine varietals to dragons or criminals, so I love the concept."

"How do you like the music? I know this isn't what you play on your radio."

"It has a good beat and a happy feeling to it. In fact, I'd like my wine and music labels to reflect happiness, so that's a start with the story."

Nathan nodded, "I can see that and design that for you. Any good news on your case?"

Jill thought about the updates and shook her head. "The valves used for arsenic are common, and frankly we don't know if the killer bought two hundred at one time or in, say, lots of ten. As they are also used to legitimately filter the water in mobile home communities in Arizona and Nevada, just buying a large shipment doesn't mean anything. So for the most part, the valve is a dead end. That said I do want to buy one tomorrow at the home improvement store close to our hotel. Maybe holding the murder weapon will inspire new thoughts about the investigation."

Nathan nodded as the musicians ended their break and the

music began again. She switched her brain to thinking about her varietals representing the instruments of a band. What kind of band was playing music for her grapes? She mostly listened to pop music, and that brought up thoughts of drums, guitars, and maybe piano. Which wine varietal would represent each instrument and why were the instruments or grapes happy? Those questions occupied her mind until her head hit the pillow in their hotel room later that night as she snuggled up to Nathan and fell asleep.

CHAPTER 18

Jill quietly crept out of bed the next morning so as not to disturb Nathan. She grabbed a sweater, blanket, and a cup of coffee from the hotel room coffee maker and made her way outside to the patio table. Nathan would likely be asleep for another hour, and it was too early to start drinking wine. She noted that the hotel would deliver room service to their patio and ordered a pot of coffee and breakfast. She was tempted to wait for Nathan, but she was hungry, and she had no idea of when he would wake up—after all, they were on vacation so there was no rush. She could also drink more coffee while he ate.

She opened her email but paused to think about Henrik's computers and his ability to tap into large datasets. What if she looked into the largest private home security companies? Would he be able to tap into their cameras and get old footage? Would he be able to do a search of when a human stood close to the water pipes for longer than, say, three minutes? That would exclude anyone just walking by as well as any water utility meter readers. It would take some time to turn off the water, then drain the water in the pipes to get rid of the pressure, then saw open the pipes, add the valve, and then wait for the pipe cement to set before turning on the water again. Their killer as far as she knew had managed to insert the arsenic-filled valves without causing water leaks. So they had skill at connecting plumbing parts.

Knowing that garbage in equaled garbage out as far as data sets, she wrote the words to refine her search for video footage. She thought about asking Henrik if his staff could hack into home video doorbells, but of the water lines she had seen so far, a doorbell camera wouldn't catch the movement of a killer as most of the water valves were placed beyond the range of a doorbell camera. So, likely the pursuit of front door cameras would lead nowhere. Next, she spent some time looking at home security systems and she checked in with the few mobile park community social media groups that she'd visited earlier in this investigation to see if anyone was talking about their community security system. She sent the parameters of the mobile home parks in question, picking just ten of them knowing that when examining video coverage the size of the data searches multiplied by large numbers.

By the time her food arrived, she had an answer to that question and Nathan surprised her by coming out to the patio. He looked at the meal that had just been delivered to her and he turned around and entered their hotel room. That was weird. Did he decide to go back to bed?

Moments later he came back out with the second coffee cup from the bathroom and poured himself a cup from her coffee carafe. He sat down, breathing in the coffee.

"You're awake early. Would you like me to order this same breakfast for you?"

He nodded, rubbing his eyes. She pulled out her phone and made the call.

"It will be here in about fifteen minutes."

He nodded without saying anything, so she went back to her laptop studying the social media groups and taking notes when security systems were mentioned. She had finished her breakfast by the time his breakfast arrived. After about five minutes of eating, he began talking.

"Any overnight news on your case?"

"Yes, but it's minimal. I'm composing an email to Henrik to see if his analysts can find cameras on any of these pipes or even on the street leading into each development. However, I learned my lesson with the last search. I need to be very specific and thoughtful about the data I'm searching for. Right now I'm searching the social media mobile home community groups to see if there's any discussion about the park's security system. I'd like to be specific by company, address, object, and date range to look for. How come you're up early?"

"I'm on vacation so I didn't stay up late working on designs, so I had adequate sleep. Did you give any thought as to which musical instruments you want on your wine labels?"

"I did. I'd like a guitar, drum set, keyboard, and two other instruments that I've haven't decided on. I need to explore the personality of these varietals to determine that."

"Personality?" Nathan asked.

"Yes. Don't you think the drum player should have a bold and energetic flavor to it? So which of my varietals is suited to that?"

"I'm not sure I've heard someone talk about the personality of their grapes."

Jill smiled at his comment and said, "That's why you're the creative dude behind labels and I'm the genius with getting my grapes to 'give it their all' and create great grape juice."

"Did you have a few mimosas before I arrived? I'm picturing you standing in your rows of grapevines and lecturing them on the importance of being earnest to give you the best flavor."

"I might try that in the spring. You know I do talk to the vines when I'm trimming them, but I haven't talked to them when I'm adding nutrients or picking the grapes. I'll start chatting with them at every stage. Does that help with your wine bottle label creation?"

"Ah, no. It's more like I'm wondering how I didn't notice this weird attribute of yours of talking to your grapevines. Do they answer back to you?"

"No. They just fall in line and try to produce beautiful grapes for me."

"This is probably why I don't talk very much in the morning; we seem to have ended up in this alternative reality where plants listen to their farmers. Maybe I'm still in bed and this is a dream I'm having. Except I can smell bacon. Weird."

Jill elbowed him in the side, all the while smiling at their nonsensical conversation.

They decided to hike a nearby area as it was too early to start wine tasting. There was a state park that had the most amazing wildflower blooms in March. Now there were no crowds and no flowers, but it was still a beautiful plateau. They returned to town for lunch at a highly recommended Mexican restaurant. After an excellent fish dish, they moved on to the next winery on Nathan's list.

This winery featured four of the five varietals that Jill was looking at expanding in her vineyard. They had a discussion about the labels the owner chose. Nathan's marketing and designing eye gave the positives and negatives for each label. "This was fun; we need to do this more often," Jill thought. She loved hearing his professional opinion about all things marketing.

At the next winery, they took a seat outside with their wine flights while Jill took the opportunity to look at her messages. They were all either texts or emails that she needed to concentrate on while reading. She put the phone face down and began sipping the first sample.

"Wow, this is awful. Let me figure out why it's awful as that's instructive."

Nathan nodded and said, "I chose this winery for that exact reason. Reviews showed that customers hated this wine, but liked other wines the winery produced; thus the crowd here today."

"It is helpful tasting a bad wine. I'll say this is bad as the tannins are overly strong, so the wine tastes too dry and vinegary. It's amazing that the reviews haven't reached the attention of the winery; as now that I look at those reviews, it's been going on for a few years, so likely more than one vintage."

"Yes, I agree with your assessment. I like dry wines, but this is so dry that the roof of my mouth feels parched. So do you know how to avoid making such a wine?"

"I think so. They're storing it in the wrong barrels at temperatures that are too warm. They could help this wine by aerating it and keeping the wine skins away from the juice. If they have barrels of the stuff, they can add two egg whites for every sixty gallons."

"Add egg whites to wine? That sounds gross, but you're the chemistry expert."

"It's the proteins in the egg whites that neutralize the tannins. I'm sure you can buy the protein separately. I don't understand why they are selling this wine. It reflects poorly on them," Jill said.

"I think it does, but I had to laugh at some of the reviews. Some people said it helped them decipher between what was a wine not to their taste, and a truly bad-tasting wine."

Jill laughed and added, "It's not going to help them sell that bottle even though they priced it at $4 a bottle. I guess I could see people buying it as a gag gift. You didn't by chance design their label? It's well done."

"I didn't design it. However, a classmate did, and he regretted putting his name on the label. This label is why I try to taste all wines that I make a label for, and if I can't taste it then I don't sign the label."

"I never thought about this, but don't most vineyards call you before they're ready to bottle it? So how do you know how it tastes?"

"I always ask to come onsite and taste it from the barrel. Even if they're not going to bottle it for sixty days, I know whether the wine is going to be good, mediocre, or bad. Don't you know that about your wines?"

"True, I do know months out how a wine is going to taste. It's interesting to learn the secrets of your profession. It's also interesting that this wine has been so bad for so long. I wonder if it is the same winemaker who has created all these wine flavors. I think I'll ask."

Jill asked the folks who were pouring wine about the history of the winery and in particular she asked for details about the wine master. It turned out that it was a relative who had since retired. Jill asked if they had gotten any feedback on the bad-tasting wine.

"We have. It's universally awful. However, we're working through five thousand bottles of wine. No one buys them except as a gag gift. It took us a while to figure out the gag angle. We go through two to three bottles a day, so I think we still have about a year to go before the bad wine runs out. Most visitors thank us as it educates wine drinkers on the difference between bad wine and wine you just don't like, so that's the story of our unique wine," the pourer said with a smile.

Jill and Nathan were soon finished with the winery and walked away to their car. He had one more winery lined up, but they both were in no hurry to taste more wine. Instead, they decided to drive over to the coast, which was about a half an hour away. Let the wind from the Pacific Ocean refresh them.

Jill read her emails on the way there, thinking about the latest news from the case. It was a painful process as she'd sneak a quick glance, catch two sentences, then she would have to follow the road for awhile to tamp down her carsickness.

Leticia said that when local authorities approached the mobile home park with the local water department and searched for additional valves, they found one additional valve at a home where the owner likely was suffering from the effects of poisoning. They had been checked out by the local hospital and would follow up the next morning with their doctor.

The special agent contacted her colleagues in the adjacent states and regions to brief them on the case and give them the coordinates to visit local mobile home communities based on the latest data run that Jill had forwarded to her. Reports were coming back to Leticia throughout the day. They were finding more victims, both dead and alive. They had quite a serial killer at work in the southwestern United States. Jill forwarded Leticia's recent update to her teammates. Sometimes pro-bono work could yield more satisfaction than a paid case, especially when you discovered the work of a serial killer and could put a stop to it.

As it was the weekend, both Jo and Marie had more time than usual to devote themselves to diving into data. Jill lucked out with this case happening at a time when they had few weekend plans. Jo had some information, but she wanted to wait until she completed her financial analysis of all the board and executive leadership. Marie was likewise searching the same group for personnel reasons and would be rendering a hire/don't hire rating for each of them.

Jill then received her reply from Henrik's people. She assumed that the FBI would be doing a similar search, but she liked to think that Henrik was faster and better than anything they could come up with. His analyst had sent her the data by each of the locations. There was a fast-moving video of the coverage for the six months prior. She was looking at visitors who made one or two stops at the mobile home park. That should eliminate visitors, delivery services, and frequent friend stops. The software then summarized a list of vehicles and drivers as the analyst applied the facial recognition software to identify people. Jill was getting excited about the potential results and kept scrolling down the attachment.

CHAPTER 19

"OMG." Jill said.

"What? Good news?" Nathan asked.

Jill was quietly scanning the results. Their suspect was disguised, as was their vehicle. They had a variety of vehicles—all of them vans, trucks, or utility trucks. All of them had a magnet square on the side of the vehicle that said Acme Plumbing. Acme as a business name was the most generic name of any business dating back to the 1940s and the Looney Tunes cartoon. With the use of the first two letters "AC," it ended up at the top of any alphabetical listing in a telephone book. Nothing said fake like the name Acme.

"Henrik's giant computer came through. I have a bunch of photos of our suspect standing near a variety of vehicles they used."

"How do you know that's your suspect?"

"Why else would they be wearing the same trappings that disguise their appearance, always have a white vehicle, and be near the pipes in the middle of the night?"

"Did the software identify him by name?"

"No, and at this point, it's *they*. I can't tell the gender of this plumber. I might be able to guess the height and weight, but that's it."

"Do any of the photos show the plumber installing a water valve? Is it the same person in multiple cities or states?" Nathan asked. Since he was driving, he couldn't see what she was looking at.

"Those are good questions, Sweetie. You're getting used to this private investigator life. Let me find the answer to your question before I forward it to other people."

Jill studied the data and decided that despite the fact she that couldn't tell anything about the mysterious Acme plumber, it was likely the same person in each picture and location, which were hundreds of miles apart. Next, she looked for evidence of the valve, but didn't see any pictures with it in hand. They were near their truck or bent over a pipe with a tool in hand that Jill guessed to be a pipe-cutting tool. Just the luck of the pictures and when satellites passed overhead. It appeared they did their work overnight, as all the pictures had the night look about them. That made sense as the folks she interviewed couldn't recall seeing anyone working on the pipes. She wondered if the time was about the same in each picture and discovered that Acme Plumbing's visits occurred between one and three in the morning. This report gave her ideas for more data, but first she needed to pass it on to her law enforcement partners.

Just then they pulled up to the beach parking lot; she wanted to sit in the car for a moment and compose emails to the special agent and the detective and discuss what was in the attachment, as well as the additional information she was going to ask for. She wondered if the FBI experts could guess the gender of the killer in the photos. She finished her message and hit Send then, got out of the car to walk with Nathan to view Morro Rock. She grabbed a jacket as the wind was whipping up on the ocean. She was glad for the fresh air as she had started to get carsick on the drive. She could never read very well while in a moving car, but it seemed urgent for her to understand the latest data report.

They took pictures and strolled the beach, and she relaxed as only one could when enjoying the rhythmic power of the ocean waves crashing nearby. She looked for a path to climb the gigantic rock containing an extinct volcano, but for ceremonial reasons only members of the local Native American tribe were allowed to climb it. It looked rather dangerous to climb, and she was never one to enjoy pitting herself against Mother Nature when the outcome could be a catastrophic fall. As they were walking back to the car, her cell phone rang, and she saw it was Leticia Ortiz.

"Hello," Jill said loudly as the wave action was loud. She would hear better once they were back inside the car.

"Where are you? It sounds like the ocean in the background."

"South of you in Morro Bay. Nathan and I are taking a short vacation in Paso Robles."

"And yet you're still getting all this work done on the case. That's impressive."

"I told Detective Greenwood that I solved 100 percent of my cases in under a month. I have a reputation to uphold. Besides, we've been saving lives by checking on these mobile home residents, so it's all good."

"I have two civilians I have worked with on cases that I wish I could convince to come to work for the FBI. We sure could use your skills."

"I assume I'm one of the two?" Jill said.

"Yes. There's a computer hacker who lives in my area by the name of Damian and he seems to be a lot like your German friend. Alas, neither of you will accept a job with us. On to business: I'd like to refine this data. Can you request that of your friend?"

"Yes. I was going to ask for more myself, but I was waiting to see if you had new information to add to it."

"Sadly, you seem to be out in front of us when collecting new data."

"Yes, but you and local law enforcement are actually saving lives by running down these locations with potential arsenic poisoning, so we need each other."

"True. I'll send you my questions in an email so that they're clear."

"Can your or Detective Greenwood's experts offer an opinion on whether our suspect is male or female?"

"Not yet."

They talked a little more about the case and ended the call.

"So was she wowed by your data?" Nathan asked, hearing only one side of the conversation. Jill often used the speaker on her phone when she was on a case so Nathan could hear the details, but with the noise of the ocean waves, she hadn't done that on this call.

"She was so wowed that she mentioned that I always had a job with the FBI if I would ever say "yes." She also mentioned a man by the name of Damian who sounds like he gives Henrik a run for the money on his computer knowledge. I'll have to let Henrik know he has a competitor in the eyes of the FBI."

"That will ruffle Henrik's ego. He likes to think he's the best in the world. Did they have a guess on the suspect's gender?"

"Not yet. Leticia wants more work done with the data, so I'll wait to add her questions to mine. I'll take care of that at our next winery. I don't think my stomach will handle a second car ride today where I'm reading and writing on my cellphone."

"My driving made you carsick?" Nathan asked with concern.

"Not your driving; it was the curvy road. Unless you were driving at perhaps walking speed, it was destined to happen, but I really needed to look at what my computer search turned up."

Nathan nodded. He knew that virtually any road or any boat could make Jill sick to her stomach. She'd vomited in the Mediterranean Sea and in an Irish crystal factory. Diesel boat fumes and Irish country roads followed by the sound of an etching drill on crystal triggered her nausea every time.

Instead, they talked about the upcoming winery and her thoughts so far on the wine varietals. Soon they were back in Paso Robles and on their way to the largest winery they were visiting on this trip.

"I like the approach from the road to this winery. Their tasting room is beautiful from the outside. Sadly, it's too ornate for my winery as I'll never produce wine on the scale of this vineyard."

"Yes, I have to agree with your assessment. This winery has been around for nearly one hundred years and has about one hundred acres of vines. They have a full range of varietals."

"Do you design for this winery?" Jill asked Nathan.

"I did one label, but as you can imagine, they have a full complement of in-house marketing folks who take care of their labels, among other needs. I designed that label perhaps fifteen years ago, so I don't think it is a vintage that is for sale anymore. The only bottles still available might be sitting in someone's cellar."

"That makes sense. What do you think of the labels that they've designed?" Jill asked. Nathan had a strong ego about his designs, but was also appreciative of another artist's cool design.

"They're good, I'll walk you through them inside. I'll wait here, while you send your messages."

"Oh my gosh, I was so caught up in our wine conversation that I forgot about the case for a few minutes. Thank you for the diversion."

Jill put her head down and read the email from Leticia. She was asking the same questions that Jill had planned to ask. She looked out the car window, asking herself if there was anything else to add or if she was clear enough in her request. She couldn't think of anything to add and just forwarded Leticia's email onward to Henrik's company. Then she added a separate message to Henrik about his competition in San Francisco.

They walked inside, and this was the first winery that had all five varietals that Jill was considering. She tasted them with the question of what she would do to improve the flavor, taking notes on each grape. She would have loved to speak to the people growing, harvesting, and aging the varietals, but in an operation as big as this winery, that would require an appointment with the individuals. She made a note on her calendar to reach out to them in the future to ask questions.

They finished their wine tasting and headed out to another amazing restaurant. This was on a farm again, but not in a winery setting. This farm raised crops and animals. At least the animals were humanely raised with large open fields. The dinner was excellent and the table companions made for interesting conversation. Jill also appreciated that this meal wasn't focused on wine pairings as she had enough wine for the day. Her taste buds were exhausted. Their dinner companions felt likewise as they also had been tasting for two days at this point.

They drove back to the hotel and had a clear night to enjoy their patio and companionship.

"Did you get any new ideas for creating labels?" Jill asked.

"Not for the labels, but I liked how the winery packaged a fictional story about the wine that coincided with the label. It was all marketing, but based on a few conversations I overheard, it worked. The story and the wine transported the drinker, and that's what we need to do for your wine."

"It's funny how you and I are tasting wine and beyond the flavor we're both focused on that extra something related to our occupations—you're looking at their marketing and I'm looking at tasting rooms, grapes, and fermentation techniques.

"Yes. I also listen to people talking about wine. Most of them are rank amateurs, which is your largest demographic. True wine connoisseurs are not paying attention at all to marketing.

The large demographic of amateurs is who buys your wines, so while a points rating with a famous wine expert is sometimes helpful with purchases, you're better off with a brilliant label and story."

"Speaking of your marketing brain, I have additional bottles of my newest varietal to sell. Do you think any of the stores in this area would be interested?"

"Yes. First, you're a California producer, and second, your wine is a less popular varietal so they're more likely to take a chance on you. I would offer them a consignment arrangement for at least one hundred bottles and deliver them here yourself. If you ship them, you're really cutting down your profit."

"That's my plan," Jill said, looking down at her phone after feeling it vibrate.

She smiled at the text and said, "Henrik wants to know the name of the guy in San Francisco and oh, by the way, my latest search results are available."

"You knew that would bug him to hear that the foremost law enforcement agency in the world thought he had an equal."

"Yes. I knew he would be perturbed on many levels, but I know he sure helps me on my cases, so I'll soothe his ego."

Jill ran through the reports and forwarded them on to Leticia. The information might be more helpful to law enforcement once they got to the conviction part of any case, but they didn't help her. She moved on to emails from Marie and Jo, hoping to find more useful information.

Although they worked separately, they both had zeroed in on the same person as the likely suspect. It was the person in charge of acquisitions. He was charged with finding new properties to buy and redevelop. Five years ago, those acquisitions took too long, and he was in danger of losing his job. At the time, his wife initiated a divorce, and he did his best to deny her alimony and child support for their two children. She apparently had a bad lawyer and received little in the divorce. She moved into one of the mobile home community properties that he was trying to acquire and joined the resident fight against him and HBX Builders.

Oh no, Jill thought; she could see where this story was going. She died about six months after the divorce and as she had seen a doctor recently and was under his care, an autopsy was not completed. The two children lived with their father for a few years but had since moved on to live with their maternal aunt. Meanwhile, their suspect had received raises and bonuses and was elevated to an executive position.

His name was Mark Jackson. He was the head of Marketing and Acquisitions for HBX Builders. Meanwhile, per Marie, her assessment was "Don't hire." He had a reputation as a womanizer and people hated working for him. He was a night owl and avoided meetings before noon. That was a rare requirement for someone on an executive leadership team, but there was plenty of gossip about that habit of his. Neither Jo nor Marie listed the ex-wife's name, so she sent an email to find that out. If she was buried and they could exhume her for an autopsy, they would probably find arsenic poisoning, though maybe he hadn't perfected his technique early on. The community she lived in was long torn down and replaced with new houses, which meant they couldn't look for evidence of the arsenic water valves.

Jill had zero evidence to link him to the case. It was a gut feeling by her trusted team members. She debated whether to forward this information to law enforcement. They placed little value in hunches, especially when those came from people they hadn't met. Still, she should have built up some bonus points given her work so far on this case. Maybe they could put a tail on the man and see if he was caught inserting additional water valves. Also, they had many fingerprints on the one water valve and maybe they could match them to his fingerprints if they were on file. She also looked up the company's address as well as that of Mark Jackson himself. If law enforcement didn't want to tail him, perhaps she could. She looked up that information before she wrote her summary email.

She decided that it was far, about 240 miles away. Both he and the company were headquartered in Bakersfield. They had additional offices around California as well as in Nevada and Arizona. She would let the plan go until she got a refusal from law enforcement to consider her idea.

She sent her summary to her law enforcement friends and called it a night on the case. She would read no more texts or emails. If they really needed her for something, they could call her on the phone. Instead she snuggled next to Nathan and said, "Even though this mini-vacation isn't over, I think we should plan our next mini-vacation. What do you say to visiting my friends in Green Bay? There are a growing number of wineries, craft breweries, and distilleries there for you to impress."

"We could do that over the holidays while I'm on a school break; how would you like to spend Christmas with your friends? We might even take in a Packers game."

"You're the best! Let me check with them to see if that works with their schedules. They all have family events, but they like to include outside people like us."

CHAPTER 20

Jill was up early on Sunday morning as usual and Nathan likely was going to sleep longer. She again ordered a carafe of coffee, but no breakfast. They had eaten big meals and drank a lot of wine yesterday and she was more parched than hungry. Today they would check out of their hotel and hit two wineries before heading home. Jill also wanted to stop at local liquor stores to see if she could sell any cases of her latest vintage.

She settled in to see what had been discovered overnight. Basically, the emails said that she hadn't convinced law enforcement that Mark Jackson was their suspect. She sighed in frustration. Her friends had found the ex-wife's name and Marie did a social media search on her. Since she was deceased for several years, her accounts were closed, but Marie was able to find information from her sister. She was buried rather than cremated. Jill filed that away for later in the case as they had insufficient evidence to exhume her at this time.

It appeared that law enforcement was burdened with assisting victims of arsenic poisoning, which should be their first priority. Then she corrected that thought—it *wasn't* a burden; they were saving lives. However, she knew how diffi-cult it would be to get water companies to test the water lines, or to convince people to get tested, especially since not all of them would be able to afford the medical bills that came with testing.

She thought about her schedule for the week ahead and it was light. Her grapes were dormant, and she had the bottling company coming on Tuesday. She could check on Mark Jackson on Monday or Wednesday through Friday. She rather liked the latter half of the week as she could stay overnight in the area, which she needed to do as he did his work at night and she would likely need to follow him around between midnight and three in the morning. However, what if he was working in an adjacent state? He couldn't spend all night driving, for example, to Phoenix to place a valve, or he would arrive beyond the set hours.

Maybe she needed to re-think that idea. If he was using a variety of vehicles, were they stored somewhere? Were the vehi-cles owned under his name? Or was he stealing them prior to committing each job? She needed to go back and study the pictures—were they all California license plates? She would back off on the tailing idea and do some more information gathering. Did Henrik or Leticia know a hacker who could get into corporate records so they might know who the targets were? Did he wait until the leadership approved a location before he planted the valves? That seemed like a rational approach. She needed more data. She was deep in thought thinking about the logistics of how Mark planned his murder schedule. He obviously wasn't placing an arsenic-laden valve every night, and for those locations farther from his home, did he wait until he had a meeting in the area and group them, or what?

Jill really needed to understand his movements. Perhaps she should start with tracking his car. To do that, she probably would need to sneak into his garage to place the tracker or do so in the parking lot of his office. She wasn't good at trying to sneak at anything and she was a lousy liar, so she needed to avoid confrontation at any cost. She did some research on whether satellite images could be used for tracking his personal car, and from what she read, probably not. She would have to ask that a satellite be moved to monitor a particular location, and she didn't have that kind of power to make such a change.

She was still thinking about her options when Nathan joined her on the patio. He'd carried a mug outside with him and reached for her carafe which fortunately had a cup's worth of liquid still inside it. He had a few sips and said, "You look pensive, and that's never a good sign. What are you up to?"

That made Jill burst out laughing, then she said, "I was trying to figure out how to track my suspect since law enforcement doesn't want to follow up on my intuition."

"That's probably dangerous. Isn't your suspect a serial killer who has made oodles of money from his company?"

"That's true, but I also can't figure out practically how to track him. He's carrying out his poisoning perhaps at a rate of one a week or even one a month. Then there's the problem that he's used a variety of vehicles that he either owns or he's stealing. Also, his work is done early in the morning. So it won't be as simple as my driving to Bakersfield tomorrow and parking outside of his house."

"You know from your experience in other cases that in the end, your intuition will be correct and law enforcement will lock him up. How about trying a different tack—can you convince law enforcement to go and interview the company that employs your suspect? After all, they should know about the trend of murders related to their properties and potential acquisitions."

Jill pointed a finger at him and said, "You are correct! I need to try that tactic. I wonder if I could join the interview."

Nathan shook his head and ordered another carafe of coffee and breakfast from room service. "For other things on our list today, we need to eat a breakfast or brunch, check out of our hotel, and hit one winery on our way home. In light of what we've already tasted, I'm crossing one of the wineries off our list. Is there anything else I should add to the list?"

"I want to stop at a few wine stores and see if I can sell any bottles from my latest vintage. I think that will probably add about ninety minutes to our time here."

"That's fine."

While Nathan went inside to shower and dress, Jill got to work on her email regarding having a conversation with HBX Builders. She asked to be included to tell her story of the discovery of arsenic in Mary Niles' remains as well as the recent stop in the mobile home park. The only thing she didn't know was the status of this recent community. Marie or Jo had verified that the other locations on the list of communities with valves were either under consideration or in the process of a sale to the company. Her latest location outside of Paso Robles lacked that company role verification. She searched social media for conversation in that community, and by the time Nathan returned smelling and looking good, their late breakfast was arriving. Jill also had her answer about the community. She added that to the email and hit Send. As it was Sunday, they likely wouldn't try to talk to the company until Monday. Nathan and Jill proceeded according to their plan. She convinced one wine store to carry her vintage and would need to drive back to the area later in the week to make the delivery.

They arrived home in the early evening to an excited dog and a nonchalant cat. They quickly unloaded the car, adding the wines they'd purchased to their wine cellar. Jill had found wine that she liked among the five varietals she planned to plant. She wanted to be able to remind herself what she liked, taste-wise, in the varietals. Before she bottled her first blend of Moscato, she must have had at least a hundred varietals of that wine. Moscato was a popular blend and easy to obtain. Her five new varietals would require her to taste them over the coming years before she would be able to harvest her first grapes from her field. It was an exercise she would enjoy.

Jill was waiting to hear a reply from her latest email to Leticia. She figured the FBI would take the lead and contact the company rather than the San Jose Police. She wondered if they planned to just show up at the headquarters or if they were making an appointment to see the CEO. She bet on an appointment as they might be at any location in their large collection of construction projects.

There was no news that evening and Jill went to bed thinking about how she might track Mark Jackson. She decided to ask her friend and security expert, Henrik, if he had any ideas on how to track her suspect. He replied with the comment that satellite images were unreliable and lacked clarity for a moving car. His only suggestion was to get a bunch of personal tracking devices and plant them on her suspect; then he advised against it as it would put her in danger.

What a way to start a Monday morning. It was interesting that he also thought she needed to get close enough to plant a bug. Maybe if she made a wine delivery to the Paso Robles liquor store on Wednesday or Thursday, she could make a side trip to Bakersfield and hope to find him. Oh well, this was all she could do for now. Time to get ready for the bottling truck on Tuesday, though she already had done all the work. Jill had her labels, corks, and foil wrappings to go over the corks. Her wine barrels were ready to be forklifted to the bottling truck, so there wasn't much for her to do there. She thought about cold calling some liquor stores to sell her current vintage to, but most stores wanted to taste the wine first, so phone calls generally didn't work. She decided to research where she would buy her vines from when she planted the additional varietals. Vines generally cost $10 each and she needed roughly one thousand per acre. So she could start searching for a vine supplier as she was looking at quite an expense to plant these new grape varietals.

Finally, Leticia emailed her. They had an appointment with the CEO on Wednesday at his office in Bakersfield. Jill was invited in case the company had any questions about where the information about them came from. So she would have to defend the work of Jo and Marie, which they had questions with. Basically, on her end nothing was happening with the case until then. She was happy that the visit was scheduled for Wednesday as she could make that stop in Paso Robles to drop off her wine afterward.

She spent the remainder of the day working on her vineyard with no new information coming from her law enforcement contacts. She checked in with her friends about a visit around Christmas and the idea was greeted enthusiastically. So she made flight arrangements and found a rental near her friends' houses.

The next morning she was excited to see the bottling truck roll up. This particular company had excellent cleanliness. She didn't want her wine contaminated by another vintage or with dirt. By noon the truck was gone, and she had boxes of her latest vintage of Nero d'Avola to sell. Using the forklift, she returned the boxes to her wine cellar, which was large enough to hold the cases of wine along with barrels of other grapes that were fermenting. The room was mostly empty save a stainless steel barrel holding her Moscato that she was using to perform fermentation experiments on the wine.

She put cases in her trunk and back seat for tomorrow's drive to Bakersfield and Paso Robles. As it was predicted to be a cool fall day, she didn't have to stack the wine in a cooler. She also had her arsenic killer case notes and data and was ready for the meeting with HBX Builders.

CHAPTER 21

Although Jill was a morning person, she was grateful that the meeting with HBX Builders wasn't scheduled until eleven o'clock. That meant she didn't have to wake up super early to make the meeting. Jill was surprised Leticia hadn't scheduled a pre-meeting somewhere in Bakersfield, but maybe it was just the two of them talking to the CEO.

She arrived at the building and looked around for someone else who might be attending the meeting but saw no one. She checked the time again and noted she was about ten minutes early. She decided to lean against her car and wait for Leticia. It was quite a haul from San Francisco—she could have flown, but with the time spent getting through an airport, it was probably a horse apiece.

She was reading her email when another car turned into the parking lot and it was Leticia and a man. They got out of their car and introductions were performed. The man was Leticia's counterpart out of the Los Angeles office. Jill realized early on that the man did not want her in the meeting. He labeled her as a civilian and therefore she had no place in a meeting with the FBI and the suspect company.

"Dr. Quint, I do have to let you know that I have advised Special Agent Ortiz that it's against agency policies to allow civilians into our work."

"Yeah, we'll just consider the extremely well-qualified doctor to be a consultant. End of story," Leticia said.

Oh my, these agents were not friends and Jill hated to be the bone of contention between them. Still, she had had enough. "Look Special Agent, I've assisted the FBI with several cases. Prior to that I was a government forensic pathologist, so I'm not the rank amateur you seem to think I am. This serial killer case wouldn't even have come to your notice if not for me. People in your catchment area would have continued to die without it coming to your attention."

He didn't respond; instead, he just headed for the entrance door and Leticia and Jill followed. Leticia rolled her eyes for Jill to see. She suspected Leticia had seen this behavior before as she was so quick to ignore it. California was a large state and was at one time the bank robbery capital of the world, so these agents probably had worked together on other statewide criminal enterprises.

They approached a receptionist and held out their credentials for her to view. She nodded and made a call. Another person arrived from a closed door at the end of the lobby and invited them inside. She showed them to a conference room with a table surrounded by twelve chairs. The walls were lined with blueprint drawings, construction projects under way, and completed subdivisions. There was one picture frame showing the black and white "before" of an obviously dilapidated mobile home community and an "after" picture in color of the new community. Jill gained an understanding of the company from that one photo—they prided themselves on turning older, low-income communities into far fancier communities. She wondered where the former residents relocated to; certainly not to the high-end subdivision. She already didn't like this company for being the potential source of a serial killer, and that one picture on the wall ended all sympathy for HBX Builders and their role in this investigation. Yeah, the company needed to make a profit, but she didn't like that their sole focus was on low-income properties that pushed people out of their forever homes.

Two men walked into the conference room. The CEO was a haughty man in his sixties and his companion was his legal counsel. That was probably a smart move when the FBI calls you up and wants to meet with you. Introductions were performed on their side, and the CEO's eyebrows raised when Leticia introduced Jill as a forensic pathologist.

"We asked to meet with you today as we have a serial killer on the loose. We have at least ten deaths and another ten people undergoing treatment who should survive."

Before Leticia could continue, the CEO broke in and said, "We're a construction company and we haven't had any deaths on any of our construction sites. What does this possibly have to do with HBX Builders?"

"Yes, well, I was getting to that before you interrupted me. Every site of the murders and attempted murders has been in mobile home communities that your company is in the process of acquiring or has closed a deal for purchase, or is under consideration by you as a possible future construction site. Your company is the only link."

That was a conversational bomb dropped in the company's conference room.

"How would you know which properties we're considering for purchase? That's private company information."

"Yes it is, except when you consider an IPO and plan to take your company public. Then you file reports that are a matter of public record. Also, every murder victim or attempted victim lived in one of the mobile home communities that you've taken over; these victims were advocating against the purchase and discussed your company at length on social media."

Jill cheered Leticia getting that dig in, but it likely sailed over the man's head. Though he was the CEO, she was betting he was no longer the brains of the operation. She tried to remember who some of the other executives were to understand if there was a family member involved.

The CEO sat there dumbfounded with nothing to say. His legal counsel spoke up and said, "You obviously cannot charge a company with murder. Do you think my client is capable of these deeds you speak of?"

"We don't know the connection between HBX Builders and the killer. We just know there is one. Your client is not going to be charged with murder today," Leticia said.

"How did these murders occur?" the CEO asked.

"Until we collect more facts about this case, we won't be revealing those details."

"So what is the point of this meeting today?"

"We wanted to notify your company of an ongoing extremely serious investigation that will result in fall out for your company. You may want to prepare for that fallout. Do you have any further questions?"

Leticia's meeting was clear and if the CEO didn't get it, the lawyer did grasp the consequences to the company as he seemed liked the sharper tool in the shed between these two.

"Is there anything that the company can investigate internally to assist the FBI?" was the lawyer's parting question as their group had stood up to exit the conference room.

"No," was Leticia's response after thinking of a few brilliant zingers. She decided it was better to hold the details close.

The three of them walked outside and paused by Jill's car.

"What did you think?" Leticia asked.

"That CEO is not the brains of the operation. You handled the conversation well as he wasn't going to be helpful, so there was no point in giving him any details. Both a son and a daughter work for the company, so let's hope the next generation is wiser. I've been thinking about how to trap the employee I think is our killer. I think we need to create a news story that gets his attention that a certain mobile home park that is under consideration with HBX has entered discussions with a competitor led by someone in that community. I would think that would be enough to make him go off the rails and plant one of his devices."

"What makes you so sure he's the suspect?" demanded Leticia's colleague.

"He's got means, motive, and opportunity. His ex-wife suspiciously dies in a mobile home park. Then he's about to get fired because the acquisition of these mobile home communities is going too slowly due to obstructions by residents. He knows which communities are on the list to be purchased by HBX Builders as he is the leader for finding the communities, and so far all locations have had a relationship with that builder. He has a weird office schedule wherein he doesn't arrive to work most days until after noon. If I was up planting a device in the early hours of the morning, I might be someone who comes to work in the early afternoon also. We have pictures of our killer doing their dirty work, but we can't identify them. He uses a different vehicle each time, and from what I can tell he randomly steals a vehicle for the job, then puts it back so the car owner never knows it's missing in the middle of the night. Finally, he worked in construction on his way through college, so he likely knows how to cut pipes," Jill said.

"So why don't we put a tracker on him and catch him in the act?"

"They've been planting these valves perhaps at a pace of one or two a month. So you could waste an awful lot of time surveilling them. I'm using the term 'they' because while I think our suspect is Mark Jackson, I don't know for sure, and those pictures could represent a man or a woman. If you plant a tracker on his car, well, he's using a different car to commit these crimes. If you put it on his person, then that needs to be in a place where he always has it with him. Thus, clothes don't work."

"Let me think about your suggestion, Dr. Quint. It has merit, but I'd like to discuss your plan more with my colleagues. If he's successful and we don't catch him at the time he inserts the valve, we could subject more civilians to arsenic. Also, how would he know who to attack in the mobile home park?"

"We could call out the rabble rouser by name. Then the FBI could plant a team at the trailer and move the resident elsewhere."

"Again, let me think about."

They talked a little more about the case, and then the two agents walked away to their vehicle. Jill looked at her watch and was happy to see it was approaching noon. She could drop her wine off at the wine store in Paso Robles by around two and head home from there. It was a long day of driving, but she thought she had made her point with the FBI, and she was selling more wine, so a positive day for both careers. Nathan was spending overnight near the university, so she would have to fend for herself for food that night.

She dropped off four cases of wine, signed a consignment agreement with the shop's owner, and was on her way back home in time for dinner. Her cell phone rang on her car's screen, and she saw the caller ID said it was Leticia.

"Hello."

"Are you home? It sounds like you're driving," Leticia said with puzzlement in her voice. Clearly, in her mind, Jill should have been home.

"After our meeting, I put on my other occupation hat and drove to Paso Robles to deliver four cases of my newest wine varietal to a store there. I'm about an hour from home."

"I forget you have another career besides catching killers."

"That's one of many reasons I don't want to work for you. Grapes are my first passion, followed closely by catching criminals."

"Yeah, about that catching criminals job, I think my colleagues and I came up with a plan based on your idea. For once you might escape a case without meeting the criminals trying to end your life."

"Tell me about your plan. I'm glad you figured something out."

"Like you suggested, we'll create some media hype around a mobile home park that is sure to reach the ears of your suspect. Our staff and the Behavioral Analysis Unit agree with your premise that this must be an insider job. There's just no other way all the arsenic-valve locations could be linked to this one company. We're going to create some press around a community that is under consideration but hasn't yet been sold."

"Have you selected the community yet?" Jill's mind was racing a mile a minute. Could this stop the sale of the community that Catherine Dobson lived in? Is that something she and her neighbors would want? They had managed to gain more payment for their homes, but all of them would still have to move out of the area. She would have to check with Jo to see if the deal was inked and there was no stopping it. Though if someone was charged with murder, she could see that invalidating the sales transaction.

"No we haven't. We would like the suggestion to come from you or perhaps Jo. Can you make a suggestion by tomorrow? We need some time to set up this scam operation."

"Let me talk with Jo and with Catherine Dobson. I'd love to save her community, but I need to understand if the purchase can be undone, and if that's something the residents want. I know she would like to stay, but perhaps some of her neighbors are looking forward to moving to a new place."

"Certainly. I'd love to pick a location in my catchment area, but I thought that transaction was too far down the road to undo it."

"I'll let you what Jo says and then perhaps you can run it by your legal eagles to understand what will happen in a criminal case against the company and Mark Jackson. I'll keep you informed as I work through the angles. It's cool if the fallout from the company could save that mobile home community from a takeover."

After Jill ended the call with Leticia, she immediately called Jo, who fortunately picked up the call.

"Did you just get home from work or am I getting you in the middle of dinner?" Jill asked, looking at her clock and thinking about Jo's activities in a time zone two hours ahead.

"You got me between work and dinner. What's up?"

"So, you know that I think their executive in charge of acquisitions is our mobile home park killer. I suggested a sting operation to catch him because we have no evidence just yet to tie him to the case. He has means, motive, and opportunity, though."

She explained what the FBI scenario was and asked about undoing the purchase of Catherine Dobson's mobile home community, or for any other suggestions.

"You could pick two locations. The real estate transaction is set to close in fifteen days for the park in San Jose, so depending on how fast your suspect strikes, the FBI could stop that transaction from going through. You could also pick a park in Phoenix that is under consideration but hasn't signed a contract," Jo suggested, giving her what she remembered of the mobile home community's name.

"That's a brilliant suggestion, Jo. Thanks!"

"I've glad for once that you're not a part of the scheme. You, your house, and Nathan should remain safe with this case."

"I hope so!"

Jill mentioned the planned Christmas visit and Jo reaffirmed that she was on board. They ended the call and she pulled over to text Leticia Jo's suggestion. Then she called Catherine's number.

"Hi Catherine, it's Jill Quint. Do you have a minute?"

"Yes, of course. How's the case going? It sounds like you've been able to save other lives from that dreadful man."

"We have. I have a question for you about your community. Would the overwhelming majority like to stay put, or are they looking forward to being bought out and moving to a new location?"

"Are you kidding? We all want to stay. We're a low-income group and all of us are facing the expenses involved with the move. If we're buying elsewhere, there are fees. We need to have help to move our belongings. Once we get to where we're going, we may need new health insurance, and we have to find new doctors. That often means paying for a meet-and-greet to establish ourselves with a new doctor. I would say that no more than one or two residents are looking forward to the move. Do you have a way to stop it?"

"I don't want to get your hopes up, but yes, there may be a possibility. I want you to keep this information to yourself for the time being. Can you do that?"

"Yes, I won't say anything as my neighbors and I have been on such a roller coaster over our future lives and I don't want to get anyone's hopes up. Do you think that if any of us spent money on a deposit or a real estate offer in another location, that we can get it back?"

"I don't know. The government has a victims' fund, and I'll find out for you."

CHAPTER 22

*J*ill ended that call and was about to call Leticia and realized she was nearly home. She'd been so involved in the case and her thoughts that her driving had been on autopilot. She would make the call once she was inside the house.

She opened a bottle of wine to breathe, then sat down at her computer to make her call. She liked to make business calls in front of her computer so she could immediately research anything related to the call.

"Leticia, I spoke with Jo and Catherine Dobson. Jo said the sale on their community closes in about fifteen days, so there is time to stop it if we manage to link Mark Jackson to the murders. Catherine indicated that community members were fretting over the move. While they are getting a sum for their home, none of them are looking forward to moving, and they're complaining about affording moving costs. So if we stopped the sale, nearly all would be happy. So here's my plan: let's get a bunch of negative publicity about this sale and one in Phoenix. The one in Arizona doesn't have a formal contract yet, so it's in a very early stage. The one in San Jose is in your territory and is in a very late stage. I would bet that we need to use a real resident's name as the company likely has the homeowners' names. I would recommend using Catherine's home. We could build a story around the fact that she was taking up the fight to block the sale on behalf of her good friend and then we need another legal group to file a lawsuit. Both of those should cause Mr. Jackson to focus on doing something in those two locations."

"That sounds like a good idea. I'll include my colleague you met earlier today as Bakersfield is in his region, but my Phoenix colleague and I will flip a coin on where our killer gets prosecuted. Remember, we not only need to link your suspect to the crime, but we need evidence to convict him which we don't have yet. I did look up his ex-wife and she was buried, so we can likely talk the family into an exhumation of her remains. This will take about a week to put in place. If he places another arsenic valve in line this week, it won't kill the resident in such a short time, correct?"

"They might suffer some damage to their organs depending on how much tap water they drink, but it shouldn't be enough to kill anyone in a week."

"Okay. I'll let you know what we're up to."

Jill ended the call and poured herself a glass of wine, placing it near a seat at her kitchen island. She searched through the refrigerator and freezer for something she could cook. She found a prepared meal and pulled that out to defrost. Then she called Nathan and left him a voicemail with her latest information about the investigation. He should be relieved that there was no part of this sting operation that put her at risk. He'd call her later that evening as he was probably meeting with a student or out to dinner with one of his colleagues.

She heated up her dinner and did some more research on the Phoenix location. The search from Henrik had found a valve at that location. No one had died yet per the local police, and the person being poisoned hadn't drunk much tap water, so she checked out clear at the hospital. Jill looked at the social media stuff for the community and it looked like they were in the very early stage of an acquisition. Though the poisoning was causing daily damage, the risk was low to the occupant due to her low consumption of tap water.

There was nothing more to do for the Mary Niles case, so she turned back to her recent vintage of Nero d'Avola. She had many cases of wine to sell. Nathan created a fabulous label for her and some marketing materials that she could hand out to stores that sold her wine. She wrote down the address for all the local wine stores within fifty miles of her vineyard. Tomorrow, she would take her varietal sample and the marketing materials and see what she could sell.

Apparently, she was free for the evening. She decided to gather more information on her new grape crops—what they would need sun wise, drainage, and nutrients. Some vines preferred to cling to a hillside and others were content being on flat terrain. Some vines liked to soak their roots in water, and others rotted when that happened. That was the challenge of being a vineyard owner. She headed to bed planning to hit the wine stores in the morning. Nathan would be back in the evening, and they could begin the reservations for a holiday visit to Green Bay.

She went up to bed early, planning to read a new urban fantasy book that was just released by her favorite author. She settled into her bed with Trixie nearby on her dog bed. She was startled out of a good story when her perimeter alarms went off. She opened her tablet to see what was going on. They'd been quiet for almost the last year. There was a person in a recognizable outfit. It was their arsenic killer, though she still could not guess at their gender.

It was good that she lived in an area surrounded by fields of grapevines, as her system was loud and bright, but she had no close neighbors for it to bother. Her phone rang and it was Nathan.

"Are you awake and okay?"

"Kinda hard to sleep through the noise and light of my security system. I was reading a good book when my alarms went off. I recognize the intruder."

"I thought you said you weren't going to be put in any danger with this case."

"Guess I shouldn't have gone to the CEO's office and been introduced by name. It wasn't too hard to find me with my unusual last name. I've got to go and deal with this; I'll call you back."

Nathan said, "Love you," and they ended their call.

She called the local sheriff's office, and their dispatch said an officer was on her way as her security company had notified them. She was unfortunately a frequent flier with her local sheriff as numerous previous murderers thought it a good idea to add her to their list. Jill thanked them and got dressed. She sent a text to Leticia about what was going on, all the while watching her suspect. She was relieved when they got into another probably stolen vehicle and drove off. She shut the noise off but left the bright lights on, just in case the suspect wanted to come back. Trixie was a high-strung dog and nervously kept to Jill's side.

Jill viewed the various cameras and noted when her favorite night shift deputy turned into her driveway. Jill had hit the button to open the gate when for the deputy. She put on a coat and went outside as Deputy Davis exited her squad car. Jill sent a quick text to Nathan about the deputy's arrival as that would ease his worries.

"My shift was cruising on in a quiet manner when I got the call from dispatch that there was activity at your winery. Imagine my surprise. Were you just missing me?"

"Yes, I'll always miss you, Deputy Davis, and in all seriousness, I need to thank you for saving my life on a couple of occasions. I don't think tonight will be one of them. The suspect has left the road."

"Suspect? What's your current case of trouble that you're involved in? Do all of your suspects take potshots at you?"

"This is a case of a suspect whom I believe to be Mark Jackson who has killed numerous mobile home park residents who resisted the sale of said mobile home park to HBX Builders. The FBI and SJPD and other law enforcement agencies are involved."

The deputy mumbled, "Of course they are." Then she said, "I'm going to drive over to where they parked their vehicle and set off your alarms. Do you and Hop-A-Cassidy there want to join me? By the way, what's your suspect's weapon choice? Gun? Knife? Strangulation? Just so I'm prepared if they are still in the area."

"An arsenic-laden water valve."

"Say what?"

"It has some heft to it, so I suppose my suspect could bash our heads in with it. He has worn outfits and driven a stolen vehicle to portray himself as a plumber. He saws water pipes apart and places a normal-looking water filter in line to the mobile home, except that he removed the carbon in the filter and replaced it with arsenic. Then the person dies in three to six weeks depending on how much tap water they consume."

"That's sick and brilliant."

"Yes, and my suspect has done this perhaps two hundred times throughout California, Nevada, and Arizona."

"Wow. You need to come and teach at the Sheriff's Academy since your cases are so strange," the deputy said as they proceeded along the dark road to the area where her suspect set off the alarms.

They arrived there and Trixie jumped out of the back of the squad car, sneezed a few times, then proceeded to search for smells. Jill didn't think the dog was smelling her suspect, but rather was scenting the normal nightlife of raccoons, possums, squirrels, and foxes. Jill walked over to where the suspect appeared on video and looked around but didn't see anything.

"See anything?" the deputy asked after also looking around.

"Nope. How about you?"

"There are tire tracks, but that's not very helpful as you can see the vehicle on your feed."

"True that."

"I don't see anything more that I can do for you tonight. Can you?"

"No. Hopefully, he was scared away and stays away. Now that I know the CEO passed my name on, I'll look every day for an arsenic valve somewhere on my property."

"Does arsenic in the water hurt your wine crops?"

"If this was the summertime, then yes. However, it's winter and we're having enough rain so that I'm not using my irrigation system. So even if he does manage to foil my security and get a valve placed on the vineyard, it won't be a problem. If he gets a new murder weapon, I might be in trouble."

"I'll drop you back at your house. Your security system covers all of your property, doesn't it? I'm just confirming that I won't get a call the remainder of my shift."

"I think you'll be free from calls related to my property. You can drop me off at my front gate."

"Was your system turned off while we went to the place where your suspect appeared?"

"I turned off the audio alarms and left the spotlights on. So if they entered the driveway or my house, I would have received notification on my phone."

"Would you like me to do a search of your residence just to be sure that the suspect didn't enter?"

Jill thought about the deputy's question. She couldn't remember any comments about Mark Jackson being a tech person, so she thought she would be safe, but it wouldn't hurt to have the deputy check her house. Certainly, Nathan would expect her to accept the offer.

"Thanks, I'd appreciate if you would take a look around. Certainly, Nathan would be pleased if I had you look. I don't see how he could have gotten in as I have such a high-level security system, but it's better to be safe than sorry."

The deputy parked her car in front of Jill's house, and she led the way up the stairs to her front door. Jill unlocked it, letting the deputy enter first. Nothing looked disturbed, and the cat was in the same position. Surely if a stranger entered, Arthur would change his position. Trixie bounded in behind them and ran upstairs. That was unusual as the dog usually stayed in the same room as Jill. The deputy searched the first floor, then went up to the second level and looked around. The dog walked all the rooms and met them as if to say it was all clear. Jill shrugged and followed the deputy hanging back in the hallway. Nothing seemed out of order or disturbed. Hopefully, the rest of the night would be undisturbed. The deputy left and Jill called Nathan first.

"So what happened?"

"My suspect, who I think is Mark Jackson, tried to enter the property through the back. It was only eleven, so that's a break in his behavior. He likes to do his valve work from one to three."

"Did you get any camera shots with him holding a valve?"

"He had a backpack, but nothing in his hands. I think my security system scared him right out of the county. Deputy Davis searched our house but didn't find anything out of place. Arthur was in the same place I left him, and surely he would have moved if a stranger came into the house in my absence.

"That's a good question about what Arthur would do. He would normally shy away from visitors to my office, but I can't recall his behavior inside my house. I'll have to bring a stranger inside and test him out. It would be good to know if he's a security cat. So you think it will be quiet the remainder of the night?"

"I do. I rechecked my file on him, and he doesn't have any kind of an IT background to try and disable my system. I think he'll stay away for now."

"What if it's not Mark Jackson?"

"That's the big unknown. We still have no proof he's the perpetrator."

"Okay, you probably have a fast-beating heart, but I'll let you go to sleep. Love you."

"Sweat dreams honey, love you back."

Jill ended the call and looked at her texts to see if Leticia responded. She saw nothing from her in text or email, so she decided not to call her as it was approaching midnight, and her news could wait until morning.

CHAPTER 23

The FBI asked for video footage of her visitor when Leticia contacted her the next day. She was concerned that their suspect was escalating by visiting Jill's house. The two FBI agents would add surveillance to their homes in case he went after them. The FBI went to great lengths to hide agent addresses, so their suspect might have a harder time tracking them down. Jill wasn't worried as she had a state-of-the-art security system and at this time of year, she had no one working in her vineyard, so she could leave the system on all day as it was trained to ignore Jill's and Nathan's faces and their cars.

The FBI was moving forward with setting up a sting for the two trailer parks. They planned to launch the Phoenix mobile home sting a week after the San Jose sting. They moved Catherine to a hotel for a week and took up living in her trailer. She was happy to cooperate as the FBI was footing the bill for the hotel as well as her food, and if this plan helped end the sale of her community, then that was an excellent thing. The FBI also had cars planted in and near the mobile home park in an attempt to catch their suspect. Now all they needed for them to do was take the bait and try to sabotage Catherine's mobile home.

Jill was still focused on Mark Jackson and wondered what he would do next. His current method of killing residents took too long for it to work to solve the problem with the closing date on Catherine's mobile home community. He needed to get the project back on schedule immediately. What would he choose as a weapon? She wondered what he had in his backpack as he needed a faster weapon to do her in as well. She re-watched the video to see if she could guess, but she didn't have footage of his loading his pack and she couldn't see a weapon on his fake uniform as it was a blob on video. It wasn't defined enough to see weapons holstered on the body.

She went back to the reviews that Marie and Jo had independently created. Despite his making more money and not supporting his children through childcare payments, he wasn't saving. She wondered if Henrik had people who could hack into his credit card accounts and see what his purchases were. Maybe he had a gambling problem, or his mortgage was consuming too much of his salary. She had no answers there, but emailed Leticia hoping that she could ask the BAU experts what his likely choice of another weapon would be.

With nothing more she could do on the case, she set out with a few samples of her Nero d'Avola vintage and her marketing materials to see if she could sell any cases of wine to nearby stores. She hated handselling her wines, but that was made easier by the fact that most store owners loved to talk about wine. By the end of the day, she'd managed to sell about 80 percent of her cases. She headed home with a satisfied glow. Then she looked in her rear-view mirror, and her attention span came to abrupt focus on the white utility van.

How long had that been there? She was still inside a nearby populated city, so she made a few random turns to see if the van was following her. Sure enough, every turn she made, the van also made. She hit the phone app on her car screen and the phone rang.

"Are you close to home?"

"Maybe about ten minutes out. Why?" Nathan said, concern in his voice.

"I have someone on my tail that I can't shake. They're in a white utility vehicle. Can you head toward Leland City and meet me here for an escort home?"

"I've already turned around. I should be there in about five minutes. Where should I meet you? Do you want me to call the police?"

"Meet me at the corner of Main and Third Street. I think I can drive around in circles until you get here. I don't know the police force in this town and I'm afraid they'll think I'm a nut case. What if the driver is innocent and gets injured from my overreaction?"

"I'm not sure that's the right answer. You keep driving and I'll call Leticia. I want you to concentrate on not letting the vehicle get too close."

Jill gave her agreement and did as Nathan suggested. If the van hit her hard, that might force her to get out of the car, especially if she had an airbag explode in her face. As she approached the suggested intersection for the third time, she saw Nathan's car a block away. Traffic was light, so he approached her car and made a U-turn, forcing the white van to brake hard and honk at him. Meanwhile Jill made two quick U-turns to pull in behind the white van. They both got out of their cars to approach the van. The driver gunned his car, drove up and over the curb, crossed the sidewalk, and went back out into the street. They could have gotten in their cars and chased him, but Jill was safe and that was all that was important.

"I guess Hollywood isn't going to hire us as stunt drivers," Jill said to Nathan after giving him a quick hug.

"More importantly, you're not harmed and neither car is

damaged. You wouldn't want to explain your second occupation to your insurance company."

"Actually, they've known from one of my earliest cases when my car got shot full of bullet holes, I think. Or maybe I didn't explain how my car got shot up, now that I think of it. We better move our cars and head home; people are driving around us."

They both got into their cars and Nathan had Jill take the front of their little procession. Jill dialed Nathan, wondering if he'd spoken with Leticia.

"Did you call Leticia?"

"No. I was driving over the speed limit and watching for cops as I didn't want to get stopped. She couldn't do much besides alerting local law enforcement here and by the time they verified her credentials, I would reach you."

"Thank you for coming to my aid. I think I forgot to say that before."

"Too bad they drove off. I was looking forward to throwing a few kicks," Nathan said, as a black belt in Hapkido.

"Yeah, well, I would rather have you safe than practicing your martial arts in a real-life situation, so I'm just fine with your skipping that opportunity. Our suspect has made two runs on me, both unsuccessful. He needs a different weapon than arsenic as it won't kill me fast enough to help with his real estate acquisitions."

"I have his license plate. Maybe the police can find the vehicle and get evidence from it."

"That's brilliant! I should have snapped a picture before I got out of the car. Send it to me and I'll call Leticia. I agree that maybe they can find the vehicle. We're close enough to home that I'll wait until we get there to call the agent."

Minutes later they were in Jill's garage. Nathan sent her the picture and she forwarded it to Leticia and then made the call as they walked into the house.

"Did you have another sighting of the suspect?"

"Yes, he started tailing me. Can you put police on alert to find the vehicle? Maybe he left evidence. Then call me back."

Jill set her phone down and went over to Nathan for a longer hug and kiss. "Thanks again for coming to my rescue. Even though he got away, I think it resolved itself in the best possible way. We're both safe. I'm sorry I keep putting your life in danger. I mean, what if he had a gun and preferred to shoot at us?"

"Yeah, I thought about that too. Just because arsenic was his thing doesn't mean he wouldn't resort to more aggression. It's why I stayed back rather than running to his car."

Jill nodded against his chest as her phone rang. It was Leticia in the caller ID.

"The vehicle was reported stolen in a town about twenty miles away. The police were already looking for it."

"Is there anything nearby that caught them on camera?"

"Good question. One of my agents is following up. Do you and Nathan need to come to one of our safe houses? They've struck at you twice in the past twenty-four hours."

"I've got a great security system here. I was out selling cases of my latest vintage of wine and was feeling a rosy glow of success. I don't know how long they had been tailing me as I wasn't paying attention. I don't know how they found me—they must have followed me from my home. Considering that I was out for perhaps six hours visiting wine shops, he had the patience to just watch and not act. By the way, I'm going to start using "he" instead of "they" as I'm convinced it's Mark Jackson even though we still don't have an ID."

"That's fine, I'll know who you're referring to. However, as the case stands at this minute, we have no evidence to charge him."

"Yeah, I know. I'm hoping that you'll find evidence in the stolen vehicle once you locate it."

"We both hope that," Leticia said as they ended the call.

"Tell me about selling your latest vintage," Nathan said, having overheard her conversation.

"I've sold about 80 percent of my cases between the shops here, in San Francisco and Paso, and the shops I visited today. Your marketing materials helped and as I told Leticia, I was so happy about my success that I must not have noticed him in my rear-view mirror until something tickled my subconscious. I've got more deliveries to make tomorrow."

Nathan had been scrolling through his cell phone while she was talking and said, "I was planning to spend the day designing tomorrow. I'll go with you for your deliveries and be your muscle."

"Are you sure? It might be an uneventful day, or they might find evidence tonight and be able to connect it to Mark Jackson."

"I'll still be your muscle. Maybe I can offer the shop owners suggestions for improving their sales, and that will make them want to sell more of your wine if they see their overall sales improve. Most wine shops at the most post the varietal, the price, and the points rating on a wine. If they would change the typeface on their shelf labels and add a few words about what each wine pairs nicely with, more bottles would be purchased."

"I'd enjoy taking you with me on a delivery and I would love to watch you work your magic on the shop owners. The shelf card you made for my vintage as well as my tasty wine was what sold them on taking a chance on me."

"Remember that, first and foremost, you have to make a tasty wine and no marketing on my part could help you sell something that tastes bad."

With a plan for the next day, Jill and Nathan decided to get a sweaty workout in before dinner. She wasn't the martial arts expert that he was as she studied Tai Chi which was far less violent than his type. Still, they had some commonalities that they could practice. After their practice, Nathan worked his usual magic in the kitchen, and they were eating when Jill's cell phone rang. She saw that it was Leticia, so she put the phone on speaker.

"My Los Angeles colleague owes me lunch," Leticia said when Jill accepted the call after apologizing to Nathan for the interruption.

"Why?"

"He thought you were an amateur sleuth for stating that Mark Jackson was the suspect."

"You found the vehicle and evidence?"

"We did. The vehicle was abandoned about twenty miles from his altercation with you in Leland City. Our CSI team swept the vehicle for fingerprints, which were on file from when he applied to the special airport security program. Rather than identifying all of the prints, we looked for just a match to him and we got it. We'll still try to match the other prints, but the vehicle's owner said that the vehicle was used by four technicians. However, they had never heard of Mark Jackson nor done work in Bakersfield, so there's no reason for him to have touched the inside of the car. He could argue that he touched the car in a parking lot or gas station, but that doesn't account for the car's interior."

"Yay to whatever law enforcement agency found the vehicle! Will you get a search warrant now?"

"We will. We'll also get an electronic surveillance warrant which will allow us to track the GPS coordinates of his cell phone. Let's hope that he used his personal cell phone when he went around installing water valves."

"Will you do a property search to see if he has any storage facilities that might contain the water valves?"

"We will do that, but it's nearly impossible to search for storage units in those mass storage complexes as there are so many of them. He could be renting one in Arizona or Nevada or somewhere in the large state of California. The phone GPS location will hopefully lead us to a storage facility."

"That sounds like great news. I hope you collect enough evidence to arrest him and get that free lunch from your colleague."

"Thanks, Jill. I hope you have a quiet night," the special agent said before ending the call.

CHAPTER 24

They had a quiet night and Nathan accompanied Jill on her deliveries the next day. Nathan was an excellent reader of people and offered his advice to the wine sellers that he perceived were open to it. He even sketched a quick and quirky label for one of the stores to use. They were finished by late morning and returned to Jill's house for lunch. Nathan would do his design work from home for the remainder of the day, while Jill was researching where to purchase her new varietal vines. It was a quiet afternoon and Nathan suggested they dine out that evening and Jill agreed. Leticia left her a message stating that the FBI still had not located Mark Jackson, and the telephone company hadn't yet compiled the location data to send to them.

They were at the restaurant when both of their cellphones went off with security alerts at home. They each looked at their phones to see what the cameras were picking up. The images looked like her suspect from the previous days. He must have studied an aerial shot of Jill's property as this time, he picked a new location to access it. They left their unfinished meals, throwing cash at their server to pay the bill and saying they had an emergency at home and rushed out to their car.

While Nathan drove, Jill studied the video. She sent a text to Leticia and called the emergency dispatcher to report an intruder at her property. She asked the dispatcher to have the deputy approach the vehicle rather than her property address and if they had a second deputy, to send them to her house. They needed to stop the intruder from getting away. Jill was grateful they were eating at a restaurant that was close to their home as they would arrive before the second deputy would reach their house. He must have been getting desperate as she would bet that the FBI and his company had made calls to him looking for him. Maybe he thought that by getting to Jill he could stop all the people charging him with crimes. Or maybe he was so angry that the gig was up for him that he wanted to get one last kill in of her. Serial killers were known to be sensation seeking, lacking remorse or guilt, and impulsive, with the need for control. They also exhibited predatory behavior. Perhaps anger and impulsiveness were controlling his current behavior.

The video showed him moving around her outbuildings. She noticed he was carrying what looked to be a gas can. Great, she had already dealt with one arsonist in a prior case. Her advantage this time was it was late fall and they had had rainfall—there wasn't dry and burnable brush lying around. He was starting to approach the house, having taken off the can's lid and started spreading gas around the house. It was normally dark except that her security system had turned bright lights on and alarms were blaring. Jill was keeping one set of fingers crossed that he didn't light the gasoline before they could stop him.

They pulled up to the house and Nathan said, "You go and get our pets out of the house, I'm going after your suspect."

Jill paused about to argue, but Nathan said, "Go! Rescue our pets!" as he took off around the side of the house smelling the gasoline.

Jill ran inside and hit the switch for the interior lights and got Trixie and Arthur and stashed them in the car. Arthur wasn't happy about the noise or lights, and she ended up with a few cat scratches. Just then a sheriff's vehicle pulled up and she hurried over to it.

"The suspect has placed gasoline around my house. Everyone is out of the house. My husband is chasing the suspect. Follow me," Jill said and took off at a run, not waiting to see if the deputy followed her.

She rounded the first corner of the house to find it empty but with the smell of gasoline, and she continued her sprint to the next side and slid to a halt. The suspect was face down on the ground and Nathan was standing near him. The gas can was out of reach of the suspect but sitting on its side.

The deputy was speaking into his communication device, and had his weapon out but pointed down. He could see this was a complex situation as he was missing so many details. His backup was on his way and would be there in a minute.

"Why is he face down?"

"I'm a black belt in Hapkido and he got a kick to his head. He's probably concussed, but our house is not on fire, so that's a win for the good guys."

The deputy walked over to the gas can with latex gloves on his hands and set it upright.

"I would have set the can straight, but our suspect isn't wearing gloves and I didn't want to tamper with any evidence."

"Did you check for a pulse?"

"No."

The second deputy arrived and the first deputy checked for a pulse. He nodded and stood up. "We'll need to call an ambulance and the sheriff as I can see this is complicated."

"Actually, the FBI is on this case. If he is who we think he is, he's a serial murderer who has been at work across three states. I'm going to call Special Agent Leticia Ortiz to inform her of this and I expect they'll be on the scene as soon as they can get here."

The other deputy sighed and said, "I'll call the sheriff, you call the EMTs. It's going to be a long night."

Soon they were both on the phone and Jill was calling Leticia. She ended the call and said to the deputies, "The FBI has a group that will arrive in about two hours as they're coming from San Francisco."

Nathan said, "I'm going to put our pets back in the house and then I'm going to water down the gasoline around the house. We have cameras everywhere, so Jill can probably find video footage of my kick to the suspect."

Jill gave him a tight hug before he walked off to do those things. He felt comfortable leaving Jill as the two deputies had their guns trained on the suspect. Though the story about this suspect was complicated, today he clearly could be charged with attempted arson and murder. Jill heard sirens in the distance and saw the flashing lights of a fire truck and an ambulance. She hadn't thought to call the fire department, but they might have a better solution for the gasoline than Nathan's plan of watering it down.

"I'll go bring these responders back here," she said, leaving to walk to the driveway.

Five minutes later, they had their suspect in a cervical collar and he was face up. Jill could see the face of Mark Jackson. Yes, Leticia was going to get her free lunch.

It was a long night between the various agencies, the interviews, and the gasoline remedy. Jill and Nathan were very grateful to have the fire personnel's expertise on the scene. The suspect was identified as Mark Jackson. The FBI had teams collecting evidence including finding information at his house that led them to his storage facility. There they found the infamous water valves and bottles of arsenic ready for use. Now someone would be reviewing all HBX acquisitions and trying to exhume remains where possible.

Other than a raging headache, their suspect didn't suffer any other damage from Nathan's kick. He recognized that the evidence the FBI had collected so far was really damning. In interviews with psychologists, he indicated he felt pressure to close on the deals for purchasing mobile home communities, especially when each community had that one stubborn person who would sway others. He did admit to killing his ex-wife, so there was no need to exhume her body. When they eventually got the logs on cell phone movements over the past five years, the FBI came up with between fifty and sixty murders and another one hundred who were sickened and hadn't died yet or had moved and were no longer exposed to arsenic.

Jackson continued targeting people as he kept getting raises and he began to enjoy the power of killing anyone just because he could. He was a true psychopath. He was trying to kill Jill as he saw her as the cause for the unraveling of all of his beautiful work. Now he would be serving a life sentence somewhere in California as that state had suffered the greatest loss of life.

Jill and Nathan gave several statements about their interactions with Mark Jackson. Jill gave Catherine a call to wrap up the case with her. She was sad that her best friend had gotten caught up in the psychopath's killing spree, but was happy to know that Mary Niles would rest in peace. She would be selling Mary's trailer which left her with an unexpected income. She was going to go on a cruise for the first time in her life. Most of all, she was thrilled that she wouldn't be forced out of her home.

Jill updated Angela, Jo, and Marie and they set dates for Jill and Nathan to visit over the holidays. She hadn't see her friends in almost six months and was anxious to relax with them. She also let Henrik know of their plans and he was planning on visiting also, so the entire gang would be together in Green Bay.

Jill received word from several wine stores that her Nero d'Avola was a hit. She purchased her vines to start growing the new crops as well as grape juice so she could start experimenting with making quality wines with those grapes.

Eventually, HBX builders filed for bankruptcy once word of Mark Jackson's actions hit the news stations. No one would do business with the company, and they were headed for bankruptcy court. There would likely be nothing left as the company was being sued in civil court in a class action suit by the families of the victims of Mark Jackson's killing spree.

Jill sat on her porch watching Trixie chase squirrels and marveled at the great life she'd been able to carve out for herself and her friends. She also felt good about taking on a pro-bono case that had turned into so much more. They'd stopped a serial killer who would have gone on for at least another decade. Yes, life was good.

The End

ABOUT THE AUTHOR

I now reside in Wisconsin, though my first 24 stories were written while I lived in Northern California. My rescue dog and cat are my companions while I write. I love to travel, play sports, read, and drink wine and beer. I enjoy the diversity of the world and I'm always watching people and events for story ideas. All of my stories are generated by my imagination, I don't use AI to write books.

If you would like to sign up for my monthly blog and announcement of new books, please follow this link: https://www.AlecPecheBooks.com

While you're waiting for the next story, if you would be so kind as to leave a review for this book, that would be great. I appreciate all the feedback and support. Reviews buoy my spirits and stoke the fires of creativity.

Readers that sign up for my blog receive a free prequel novelette for the Jill Quint Series.

ALSO BY ALEC PECHE

<u>Jill Quint, MD Forensic Pathologist Series</u>

Time's Up (prequel short story)

Vials

Chocolate Diamonds

A Breck Death

Death On A Green

A Taxing Death

Murder At The Podium

Castle Killing

Crescent City Murder

Sicilian Murder

Opus Murder

Forensic Murder

Return to the Scene of the Crime (short story)

Embers of Murder

Ashes to Murder

Mint Death

Poisonous Murder

<u>Damian Green Series</u>

Red Rock Island

Willow Glen Heist

The Girl From Diana Park

Evergreen Valley Murder

Long Delayed Justice

Emerald Bay Murder (2025)

<u>**Michelle Watson Series**</u>

Now You Don't See Me

Where Did She Go?

How Did She Get There?

<u>**Dog Humor**</u>

Eat, Play, Poop: Letters to my parents from camp

<u>**A. Peche**</u>

<u>**New Urban Fantasy Series - Stephanie Jones**</u>

The Awakening at Lake Tahoe (short story)

Witch's Medicine

Witch's Quest (2025)